U0018043

實用外交文牘
（增訂本）

PRACTICAL DIPLOMATIC
CORRESPONDENCE
(REVISED EDITION)

劉振鵬 編

BY CHARLES P. LIU

中華書局印行

CHUNG HWA BOOK CO., LTD.

TAIWAN

PREFACE

I have known the author of the present volume for close to twenty years, during which time I have learned to respect him not only as a serious student of international relations, but also as a man of uncompromising integrity.

After graduating from the National Tsinghua University in 1938, he served in the Ministry of Foreign Affairs from 1939 to 1943 when he was appointed Vice Consul of the Chinese Consulate–General in Johannesburg, Union of South Africa. He resigned this post in 1945 to do graduate work first at the University of Wisconsin and later at Columbia University where he obtained his M. A. Degree in 1947.

Upon his return to China, he rejoined the Ministry of Foreign Affairs, serving as Section Chief and later Deputy Director of the Information Department. From 1953 to 1962, he served as Counselor of the Chinese Embassy in Turkey, Counselor of the Chinese Embassy in the Philippines and Minister–Counselor of the Chinese Embassy in Greece. He is presently on home assignment in Taipei.

The present work is the result of many years' experience and painstaking effort on the part of the author. It is highly recommended not only for those who are already in the diplomatic service of the government or who are seriously interested in serving the government in the diplomatic field, but also those among the general reading public who are interested in tne conduct of international affairs.

SAMUEL C. H. LING

1963

實用外交文牘 (增訂版)

劉振鵬　編著

　　自本書在兩年前出版後，風行一時，現在爲應各方之要求，決再發行增訂版。在增訂版中除保全原書，着重示範性質的英法文文牘格式外，並增加了許多極有用處的中英文外交文牘實例，在目次及書中有關部份加註英文說明，尤其重要的是在書末添了附錄一章，編著者花了許多時間，參考了不少書籍，選編了許多常見而必要的外交名詞，每個名詞都以簡單扼要的詞句加以解釋，洵爲我國前所未有的有關外交文牘的出版物，爲各大學外交系，外文系及從事外交工作人士的最理想最實用之案頭參考用書。

序

　　劉振鵬先生早歲畢業於北平國立清華大學，其後游學美國，在哥倫比亞大學獲有碩士學位。他求學的興趣在政治學，專研國際關係。學成之後他參加高考外交官領事官及格後卽進外交界服務，先後外放南非，土耳其，菲律賓，希臘等國。多年以來，他在公餘之暇隨時隨地蒐集有關外交的資料，先後編成「外交掌故」，「實用外交文牘」兩本書，在臺北出版，風行一時。中國的外交近年來極端活躍，中國不但參加許多的國際組織，經常派遣代表出席各項國際會議，中國在外國所設的使領館單位之多，用人之衆，也是空前的。中國政府需用大批有專門訓練的外交人才，劉先生所編的「實用外交文牘」一書正是訓練此項人才最好的一種參考書籍。

　　有人也許認爲這本書裏的資料不過是外交上所通用的公文程式，其中有許多套語，好像中國公文中的「等因」「奉此」，甚至有點像中國舊式的訃聞，裏面有許多廢話，理應省除。這種看法不能說沒有道理，但是在外交上這些套語沿用已久，有志從事外交者自應予以熟習。好在這些程式並不艱深，只要文字通順很快就可以運用自如。何況我們現有劉先生這本書可以放在案頭，隨時參考，更是十分利便。

　　從事外交工作自然不只是熟習套語程式便可了事。外交文牘最重要的部份仍是其內容。怎樣可以將案情說得條理分明，使得對方徹底瞭解因而產生同情，當然是外交文牘最主要的作用。通常對於外交有兩種恰恰相反的誤解。一種誤解以爲辦外交所用的都是「外交辭令」，而「外交辭令」則是些圓滑而不着邊際的術語。外交是一種專門技術，自有其一套術語，爲外交家所經常應用。但是這些術語的含義是非常確切的，沒有被誤解的可能。舉一例來說：外交談判得不到協議，甚而談判破裂，終結時的公報往往用「共同同意不能同意」的字樣。這一句話乍看來似乎很離奇，但在懂得外交術語的人看來則是非常肯定清楚的。

— 1 —

另外一種誤解是以爲在外交上，尤其是在國際會議席上，倘若他國代表用粗暴的語言罵你，你必須「以牙還牙」，用同樣粗暴的語言反罵他，否則你便吃了虧。西洋外交史上有一個很著名的實例，係十六世紀一位俄國代表致土耳其國王的一道諜文。文中這位俄國代表所用罵人的字眼很多是粗暴到不便引用的，其勉可引用的，如「魔鬼的伙伴」,「笨豬」,「雜種」,「狗養的」，也實在不堪入耳。在外交上破口罵人可以說是俄國的傳統，不但這位十六世紀的俄國代表成爲千古的笑柄，就是今天在聯合國及其他場合俄國和其他共產國家的代表仍一貫使用粗暴的語言參加辯論。但是今天是比較文明的世界，除了俄國和其他共產國家的代表以外，再沒有人在外交上破口罵人，粗暴的語言尤爲禁忌。使用外交術語的妙處就在可以不用粗暴語言而一樣可以得到在辯論上獲致勝利的效果，而同時又可以保持一個決決大國代表的風度與尊嚴。怎樣可以獲致這樣的效果就要看這位代表能不能妙用外交術語了。

　　劉先生所編「實用外交文牘」一書增訂再版，承他不棄囑爲作序。我除了介紹本書以外又說了些別的話，其用意是希望劉先生今後更能够編一部外交文牘的示範選集，藉使有志外交工作者，除了看到外交文牘的程式以外，並可看到標準外交文牘的內容。劉先生從事外交工作多年，學識湛深，經驗宏富，再編一部外交文牘示範選集，在他該是輕而易舉的事，其價值則眞是無窮的了。

陳之邁　一九六六

增訂版序言

本書自初版印行後，自己從未感到滿意，然仍得到各方許多的關切支持與鼓勵，尤其是曾在外交界服務或現正在外交界服務的許多長官朋友的熱烈支持，指導和切實建議，如曾任駐澳大利亞國大使現調任駐日大使陳之邁先生就是其中之一，在我們好幾次的通信中他曾說過下面一段話。

"竊以爲從事外交工作進一步之練習，爲在文牘中用適當之語言將一件事說得清楚明白，旣不宜過分渲染舖張，慷慨激昂，有類政客競選之演說（此爲大忌），同時對於本國政府立場又說得絲毫不差，恰到好處，俾能收到說服對方之效果，此爲外交文牘中最困難之一種，從事外交工作者自應在此特別用功"。他在另一次信中又說過："近年來外交文牘趨向簡化，繁文儘量減少，此一趨勢美國最爲明顯。"這些話眞是至理名言。

因爲他的許多鼓勵和指點，我決定將原書加以增訂，當然我也參考了其他朋友的建議，結果我認爲應將增訂範圍擴大爲下面幾項：

一、除保全原書着重示範性質的文牘格式外，並利用目前可能搜集而且業經發表過的一部份資料，如美國國務院自第二次世界大戰以來所編行的 Foreign Relations of the United States, Diplomatic Papers 中有關文牘，我在此書中選了幾篇用作示範。

二、也有人建議文牘中應增補一部份中文的實例，使初習外交文牘者亦知中文措詞之美麗簡潔，這個我也照辦了。

三、爲便利外籍人士購置此書時檢查容易起見，特將書中"目次"及有關部份加註英文說明。

四、書末附錄一節增加兩部份資料：一爲外交名詞選編，將重要外交名詞及關係名詞選集，逐項加以簡單而扼要之說明。一爲外交上常用之尊稱。關於註釋若干外交名詞，我除參考目前可能找到的一些有關外交名詞書籍外，還翻閱了幾部國際法的書籍。

　　講到外交上的措辭，有位曾經從事外交工作的學者發表了很多極有價值的意見，我想我應該將其大意摘下來供大家參考。他說如果一位政治領袖或外交官通知另外一個政府，說他的政府 cannot remain indifferent to 某種國際爭執，這是明白表示他的政府將對這種爭執加以干涉。如果他說 His Government views with concern 或者用 views with grave concern，這表示他的政府對此事將採取強硬措施。

　　若類似這樣的警告不為對方所注意，他可使用另外一類詞句，如 In such an event, His Government would feel bound carefully to reconsider its position, 或 His Government feels obliged to formulate express reservations regarding…. 或 His Government will not allow…，或責難對方某種行動 as an unfriendly act, 這些話充分表示兩國邦交將趨於惡化。

　　本書經過了這般的增訂後，我相信更有助於從事外交工作或研究外交這門學問的人員的參考和實用。最後我要在此鄭重的謝謝所有直接間接幫助我鼓勵我的長官和朋友，尤其是陳大使之邁先生，他對我這本書增訂版的關心和指點，使我特別感激。

劉振鵬 1966

目　　次

Table of Contents

一、說　明

General Remarks

（一）外交上所習用之文字，初爲拉丁文，至十五世紀末，十六世紀初，法文逐漸使用。從十八世紀開始，英文開始兼用，今日則英法兩種文字語言均通行。在若干國家時至今日，仍有在其國內專使用本國文字，以爲外交上行文之工具者，亦有於本國文字之外，遇重要複雜案件，爲免對方誤解起見另加英文或法文譯本者，此種辦法係由於傳統慣例如此，或由於其他原因，因本書篇幅關係，不擬在此加以論列。故本書擧例時仍遵照慣例，僅採用英法兩種文字，以期其實用而便利參考。

（二）本書僅涉及外交上一般習用之文書、如國書、照會、節略、備忘錄、換文等，至於條約 TREATY、專約 CONVENTION、協定 AGREEMENT、議定書 PROTOCOL、公同宣言 JOINT DECLARATION OR COMMUNIQUE、宣言或聲明書 DECLARATION OR STATEMENT、批准書 RATIFICATION 等類文書，可在各種條約專輯或其他書冊中查得，故不再選入，以免重複。

（三）本書選輯之文書着重公文格式，故均係簡明而實用之外交文書，凡較長之公文，或因其內容無關，無助於一般外交公文之研習，或事涉機密者，概未選入。

（四）編者在外交界服務有年，最初曾利用公餘之暇試圖搜集外交文牘資料，以資自習，久之成冊，旋因國家局勢及個人情況一再變遷，資料遂告散失。至一九五三年編者奉派再度出國赴駐外各大使館服務，公餘得暇，遂又舊調重彈，時日旣久，乃有此書之編成，以視舊作，自問略勝一籌，然仍不敢自信，謹暫將之印行，以就正於外交界之先進及社會明達。

（五）書中若干說明解釋，係參考外交慣例亦根據編者個人平日之研究體認，或仍有不符理想之處，還請讀者賜予指導，他日如有機會再修正時當可獲益不淺。

（六）本書編成之後，曾請外交部參事凌崇熙先生作序，應特誌謝

（七）茲先將照會、換文、節略及備忘錄四種文體格式，分別說明如次：

（一）照　　會

Notes

照會通稱 NOTE，爲目下通行之外交文書中最正式之文件，可用第一位人稱，亦可用第三位人稱，但習慣上多用第一位人稱，因用第三位人稱其格式語調則略嫌生硬，茲爲供讀者參考起見，仍將 1909 年德國駐維爾納大使復奧匈帝國外交部照會（用第三位人稱）舉例如下：

The Imperial and Royal Austro-Hungarian Government having informed the Imperial German Government of the signature of the Protocol relating to Bosnia and Herzegovina, which has been concluded with the Sublime Porte, and having further requested assent to the abrogation of Article 25 of the Treaty of Berlin, the undersigned Imperial German Ambassador, under instructions from his Government, has the honour to make known to His Excellency Baron von Achrenthal, the Imperial and Royal Minister of the Imperial and Royal House and of Foreign Affairs, that the Imperial Government formally and without reserve gives its assent to the abrogation of Article 25 of the Treaty of Berlin.

The Undersigned, etc.

Von Tschirschky

Vienna, April 7, 1909.

His Excellency Baron von Achrenthal.

照會須由負責主持部或館務之部長或大使，公使或代辦簽名（全名），不必再加蓋部或館印，論習慣簽名之下亦不必用打字機打本人姓名及官銜。但如大公使於簽名之下，欲再將姓名及全銜（如特命全權大使爲 AMBASSADOR EXTRAORDINARY AND PLENIPOTEN-

TIARY, 特命全權公使爲 ENVOY EXTRAORDINARY AND MINISTER PLENIPOTENTIARY, 臨時代辦爲 CHARGE D'AFFAIRES a.i.） 斟酌情形打在公文上亦可，惟不宜在自己姓名前加 H. E.(HIS EXCELLENCY) 一類字樣，如自己有博士學位銜，亦不宜在簽名處寫 H. E. DR.……。此處所謂斟酌情形，即有些文件簽名，不必將姓名打上，如呈遞國書後通知各有關使館之文件，如平時離開駐在國及假滿返任一類之通知行文，不必將全銜打上，簽名即可。因通知到任之文書，已在文中說明自己之官銜等。

照會末段慣例用下列一類詞語，如英文用 I AVAIL MYSELF OF THIS OPPORTUNITY TO EXPRESS TO YOUR EXCELLENCY THE ASSURANCES OF MY HIGHEST CONSIDERATION. 或 ACCEPT, EXCELLENCY, THE RENEWED ASSURANCES OF MY HIGHEST CONSIDERATION.

法文用 VEUILLEZ AGREER, MONSIEUR LE MINISTRE, LES ASSURANCES DE MA TRES HAUTE CONSIDERATION. 或 AGREEZ, MONSIEUR LE CHARGE D'AFFAIRES, LES ASSURANCES DE MA CONSIDERATION LA PLUS DISTINGUEE.

茲舉兩例如次，一爲美駐法大使致法外交部之英文照會，一爲中國外交部長致外國外交部長之中文照會格式。

例　　一

Excellency:

Acting under instructions from my Government, I have the honor to transmit a communication on behalf of my Government to the Government of France relating to political principles which the Government of the United States considers should govern the treatment of Germany in the initial control period. It is the earnest wish of my Goverment that the Government of France will be able to associate itself with

— 3 —

these principles.

Your Excellency will note that my Government will be grateful if the Government of France would treat the present communication as strictly secret until such time as an official statement is issued by the Conference.

I avail myself of this opportunity to express to Your Excellency the assurances of my highest consideration.

....

例 二： 照 會

接准

貴部長本年　　月　　日第　　號照會內開：

『……………………………………』等由。

本部長對於

貴部長上開照會所載各項均已敬悉，並經分別辦理。相應覆請

查照爲荷

本部長順向

貴部長重申最崇高之敬意。

此致

………………外交部部長

中華民國外交部部長…………（簽名）

中華民國……年……月……日　　於臺北

（二）換　　文
Exchange of Notes

換文之格式與照會同。所約定之事情均係事先商妥，雙方同意用換文形式達成協定目的，去文與復文均事先準備於約定之日交換，復文例將去文主文重述，然後表示同意。茲舉例如次：

例一： 西班牙駐義大使致我駐義于大使照會

關於西班牙政府與

貴大使所代表之中華民國政府恢復正常關係事，本大使茲謹向

貴大使聲述：

貴大使奉有全權證書及必要之資格以進行初步談判俾達成上述目的一節，業經轉陳本國政府。

本大使茲謹代表本國政府奉達

貴大使：西班牙政府與中華民國政府同一意願，同意恢復兩國正常外交關係，並即互派大使級外交代表。

本大使順向

貴大使重表崇高之敬意。

此致

中華民國駐義大利國特命全權大使于焌吉閣下

桑格洛尼茲侯爵（簽字）

公曆一千九百五十二年六月二十八日　　於羅馬

我駐義于大使復西駐義大使照會

頃准

貴大使一九五二年六月二十八日照會內開：

「關於西班牙政府與……………………」等由。

本大使茲代表中華民國政府表示同意

貴大使來照所述之辦法。

本大使順向

貴大使重表崇高之敬意。

此致

西班牙國駐義大利國特命全權大使桑格洛尼茲侯爵閣下

于焌吉（簽字）

中華民國四十一年六月二十八日　　於羅馬

例二： 中國外交部長致泰國駐華使館臨時代辦照會

逕啓者：查本部近曾與

貴代辦就所請特准暹羅太平洋海外航空公司於其經營之曼谷——香港
——臺北——東京航線上，在臺北作臨時商業降落一事，舉行商談。
在商談過程中，已獲致下列諒解：

　一、………………………………

　二、……………………………

本部長望

貴代辦能代表泰國政府證實上述諒解。此項諒解如荷證實，本照會與
貴代辦之復照即構成中華民國政府與泰國政府間之臨時協定。此項臨
時協定應自本日起生效。

本部長順向

貴代辦重表敬意。

　　　此致
泰國駐華大使館臨時代辦…………先生

　　　　　　　　　　　　　　　　　…………（簽字）

中華民國……年……月……日　於臺北

泰國駐華使館臨時代辦復中國外交部長照會

逕啓者：接准

貴部長本日照會內開：

　『查本部近曾與………………應自本日起生效』等由。

本代辦茲謹證實：

貴部長來照內所紀錄之中國政府之諒解，亦即泰國政府之諒解。

本代辦順向

貴部長重表崇高之敬意。

　　　此致
中華民國外交部部長…………閣下

　　　　　　　　　　　　　　　　　…………（簽字）

公歷…………年……月……日　於臺北

....

Sir,

During the negotiations for the Treaty signed today between His Excellency the President of the National Government of the Republic of China and His Majesty the King of Great Britain, Ireland and the British Dominions beyond the Seas, Emperor of India, for the United Kingdom of Great Britain and Northern Ireland and India, a number of questions have been discussed upon which agreement has been reached. The understandings reached with regard to these points are recorded in the annex to the present Note, which annex shall be considered as an integral part of the Treaty signed today and shall be considered as effective upon the date of the entrance into force of that Treaty. I should be glad if Your Excellency would confirm these understandings on behalf of His Majesty's Government in the United Kingdom.

I avail myself of this opportunity to renew to Your Excellency the assurance of my highest consideration.

(sgd.) CHINESE FOREIGN MINISTER

His Excellency

Sir·······················,

His Majesty's Ambassador,

....

復　文

....

Sir,

I have the honour to acknowledge receipt of Your Excellency's Note of today's date reading as follows:

"During the negotiations for the Treaty signed today between His Excellency ...... I should be glad if Your Excellency would confirm these understandings on behalf of His Majesty's Government in the United Kingdom."

I have the honour, on behalf of His Majesty's Government in the United Kingdom, to confirm the understandings reached between us as recorded in the annex to Your Excellency's Note, which annex shall be considered as an integral part of the Treaty signed today and shall be considered as effective upon the date of the entrance into force of that Treaty.

I avail myself of this opportunity to renew to Your Excellency the assurance of my highest consideration.

(signed) BRITISH AMBASSADOR

His Excellency
　Dr. ....
　　Minister for Foreign Affairs of the
　　Republic of China,
　　　....................

....

Monsieur le Ministre,

I have the honour to refer to the conversations recently held between the representatives of the Governments of the Republic of China and Japan regarding the scheduled air services between and beyond both countries, and to confirm, on behalf of the Governments of the Republic of China, the following arrangements agreed upon in the course of these conversations, which the Governments of both countries undertake to apply within the limits of their administrative powers:

1. ....

2. ....

I have the honour to request Your Excellency to be good enough to confirm the above-mentioned arrangements on behalf of the Government of Japan.

I avail myself of this opportunity to renew to Your Excellency, Monsieur le Ministre, the assurance of my highest consideration.

(Signed).................................

His Excellency

Mr.......................

Minister for Foreign Affairs

....

復　文

Monsieur l'Ambassadeur,

I have the honour to acknowledge receipt of Your Excellency's Note of today's date reading as follows:

"I have the honour to refer to the conversations recently held between the representatives of the Governments············"

I have the honour to confirm the arrangements set forth in Your Excellency's Note on behalf of the Government of Japan.

I avail myself of this opportunity to renew to Your Excellency, Monsieur l'Ambassadeur, the assurance of my highest consideration.

(signed)·······························

His Excellency

Mr. ····················

Ambassador of the Republic of China

·····················

例　　五

Ottawa,⋯⋯⋯⋯⋯⋯⋯⋯⋯

Sir,

With reference to recent conversations between representatives of the Government of Canada and the Government of the United States of America regarding the extension to individuals ordinarily resident in Canada who are nationals of the United States and are not British subjects of certain exemptions from orders and regulations now or hereafter in force respecting the acquisition and disposition of foreign currency and foreign securities, I have the honour to propose an agreement concerning these exemptions in the following terms:

⋯⋯⋯⋯⋯⋯⋯⋯⋯⋯⋯⋯⋯⋯⋯⋯⋯⋯⋯⋯⋯⋯⋯⋯

I have the honour to suggest that if an agreement in the sense of the foregoing paragraphs is acceptable to the Government of the United States this note and your reply thereto in similar terms shall be regarded as placing on record the understanding arrived at between the two Governments concerning this matter.

Accept, Sir, the renewed assurances of my highest consideration.

⋯⋯⋯⋯⋯⋯⋯⋯⋯⋯⋯⋯⋯⋯

for Secretary of State for External Affairs.

Hon.⋯⋯⋯⋯⋯⋯⋯⋯⋯

Minister of the United States,

Ottawa.

例　　六

換文亦有不用照會，而用節略者其格式雖不同，然其目的則一，茲舉例如次：

The Embassy of the United States of America presents it's compliments to the Ministry of Foreign Affairs of the Republic of China and has the honor to request the concurrence of the Government of the Republic of China in the following understanding in regard to currency of China paid to the Development Loan Fund:

The Government of the Republic of China agrees that any currency China paid to the Development Loan Fund, an agency of the Government of the United States of America, pursuant to any transaction entered into by the Development Loan Fund under the authority provided in the Mutual Security Act of 1954, as it is or may hereafter from time to time be amended, shall be recognized as property of the Development Loan Fund. The Government of the Republic of China further agrees that such currency may be used by the Development Loan Fund or by any agency of the Government of the United States of America for any expenditures of or payments by the Development Loan Fund or any such agency, including any expenditures of or payments by the Development Loan Fund for purposes of transactions authorized by the Mutual Security Act of 1954, as it is or may hereafter from time to time be amended. Unless agreed to in advance by the Government of

Republic of China, such currency shall not be used by the Development Loan Fund or any other agency of the Government of the United States to finance exports from China or its territories nor shall it be sold for other currencies to entities other than agencies of the Government of the United States. The Government of the United States agrees that it and the Development Loan Fund will take into account the economic position of China in any comtemplated use of currency of China received by the Development Loan Fund.

Embassy of the United States of America,

Taipei, December 24, 1958.

復　文

The Ministry of Foreign Affairs of the Republic of China presents its compliments to the Embassy of the United States of America and has the honor to acknowledge receipt of the Embassy's note No. 9 of December 24, 1958, reading as follows:

"The Embassy of the United States of America ············"

In reply, the Ministry has the honor to signify on behalf of the Government of the Republic of China its concurrence in the understanding set forth in the aforesaid note.

Ministry of Foreign Affairs,

Taipei, December 24, 1958.

中 美 換 文

美利堅合衆國大使館茲向中華民國外交部致意，並請中華民國政府關於給付開發貸款基金之中國貨幣事，就下列了解，予以同意：

中華民國政府茲同意：凡因開發貸款基金（該基金係一美國政府機構）依照一九五四年共同安全法案或其嗣後修正案授權所成立之任何交易事項，而給付該基金之任何中國貨幣，應認為開發貸款基金之財產。 中國政府同意：該項貨幣得由開發貸款基金或美國政府任何機構作該基金或該機構任何開支或付款之用，包括開發貸款基金因依照一九五四年共同安全法案或其嗣後修正案下授權經辦交易事項之任何開支或付款。該項貨幣，除經中國政府事先同意外，開發貸款基金或美國政府任何其他機構不得用以採購物資自中國或其所屬領土輸出，並不得將此項貨幣售予非美國政府機構之組織，換取他種貨幣。美國政府茲同意：美國政府及開發貸款基金於策劃開發貸款基金所得中國貨幣之用途時，應對中國之經濟狀況予以顧及。相應略請查照。

西曆一九五八年十二月廿四日 於臺北

復 文

中華民國外交部茲向美利堅合衆國大使館致意並聲述：案准大使館本年十二月廿四日第九號節略內開：

「美利堅合衆國大使館茲向中華民國外交部致意，並請…………應對中國之經濟狀況予以顧及」。等由。

外交部茲代表中華民國政府對上述節略所提了解，表示同意。相應略復查照為荷。

中華民國四十七年十二月廿四日 於臺北

復　文

Ottawa, Canada, ·······························•

Sir,

I have the honor to refer to your note of today's date proposing an agreement between the Government of the United States of America and the Government of Canada concerning the extension to individuals ordinarily resident in Canada who are nationals of the United States and are not British subjects of certain exemptions from orders and regulations now or hereafter in force respecting the acquisition and disposition of foreign exchange and foreign securities in the following terms:

··

I have the honor to inform you that an agreement in the terms of the foregoing paragraphs is acceptable to the Government of the United States of America and that this note, and your note under reference, will be regarded as placing on record the understanding arrived at between our Governments concerning this matter.

Accept, Sir. the renewed assurances of my highest consideration.

································

The Right Honorable
　　The Secretary of State
　　　for External Affairs,
　　　　Ottawa.

（三）節　略
Memorandums

我國所稱節略之外交文件，西文之稱謂不一，有稱 MEMORAN-DUM 者，有稱 NOTE VERBALE 者，有稱 AIDE MEMOIRE 者，有稱 NOTE CIRCULAIRE 者。普通寫明 CIRCULAIRE 者多係一種油印文件，如通知館址更動，或電話號數變更等一類瑣事。亦有稱 THIRD PERSON NOTE 者，因此項文件措詞從頭至尾，均係用第三位人稱，故有此稱謂。日本慣稱 Memorandum 爲"覺書"。

節略之使用範圍甚廣，凡平時不宜用照會之文書，均可使用節略，如洽商外交上之普通事件，如通知館員到任，或館長短期離館，或館長或使館更改住址，改裝電話等例行事件皆屬之。收到此類文書有用節略復文者，有不復者，一切視駐在地慣例及事情之性質而定。

節略不一定由館長簽名，可由主辦人或使館中指定之館員一人負責 INITIAL（即簽其姓名之首字母）即可，INITIAL 之後加蓋使館圓章，INITIAL 可在全文最後一段之尾爲之，亦可在文下空白之適當處爲之，如採取後一種辦法，使館圓章即可在簽字上加蓋，不可在節略之下先打本人姓名官銜再行簽名，如此似不合慣例。

如爲極普通之例行通知，用油印通知同駐在地之各國使館者，蓋一使館圓章即可，毋須 INITIAL。

節略最後一段有照例加客氣語一段者，如英文加 THE CHINESE EMBASSY AVAILS ITSELF OF THIS OPPORTUNITY (OCCASION) TO RENEW THE ASSURANCES OF ITS HIGHEST CONSIDERATION, 法文加 L'AMBASSADE DE CHINE SAISIT CETTE OCCASION POUR RENOVELER AU MINISTERE DES AFFAIRES ETRANGERES LES ASSURAN-CES DE SA TRES HAUTE CONSIDERATION. 此類套語若干國家行文時亦有不加者，在節略中應洽商或請求或說明之事件說明清楚，節略正文即告結束，不再加上述套語，論一般外交行文慣例，

加與不加均無不可，應注意者宜符合當地習慣，適應駐在地環境，如駐在地喜用此類套語，認爲加後可以增加該公文之美麗，加亦無妨。

正文之後有附件者，註明附件，或寫 Enclosures: As Stated. 最後打發文之城市名及年月日。

例 一

MEMORANDUM

The Ministry of Foreign Affairs presents its compliments to the Embassy of ………… and has the honor to refer to the Ministry's memoranda to the Embassy dated September………, 1956, and November…………, 1956, regarding the transfer by of the ………… to …………, in which the Ministry repeatedly expressed the position consistently held by the Government of ………….

In view of the declaration made by ………… the Ministry wishes to reiterate the views of the Chinese Government on the status ………… as follows:

1. ………… …………

2. …………………………

3. …………………… Any solution of this question without prior consultation with the Chinese Government would be considered not acceptable. The ………………… Government is therefore requested to give this matter reconsideration in the light of the views stated above.

Taipei, February …………, 1958.

節　略

外交部茲向………大使館致意，並願提及外交部於一九五六年九月〇日及同年十一月〇日先後送致大使館之備忘錄，就………事送向大使館闡明中國政府之立場。

鑒於………外交部茲重申中國政府對於………之意見如下：

一、………………

二、………………

三、………………關於此項問題之任何解決，如未經與中國政府事前磋商，將視為不能接受，爰請………政府就上述各項意見，對此事重加考慮。

中華民國〇〇年〇月〇日　　於臺北

例　　二

L'Ambassade de Chine présente ses compliments au Ministère des Affaires Etrangères et a l'honneur de porter à Sa connaissance que le Ministère de l'Education de la République de Chine, dans le but de promouvoir les relations culturelles avec les pays amis et pour faciliter l'étude de la culture chinoise aux étudiants ressortissants de ces pays, a créé des bourses pour étudiants étrangers.

Cette Ambassade fait parvenir sous ce pli au dit Ministère une copie en double du règlement régissant l'octroi de ces bourses et Le prie de bien vouloir porter ce qui précède à la connaissance du Ministère ………de l'Education Nationale.

L'Ambassade de Chine saisit cette occasion pour renouveler au Ministère des Affaires Etrangères les assurances de sa très haute considération.

Annexes: 2

……………… 1959.

Ministère des Affaires Etrangères
EN VILLE

（四）備　忘　錄

Aide-memoire

備忘錄法文稱 AIDE MEMOIRE 英文稱 MEMORANDUM，此項文件無一般文件中所習用之頭尾，亦不用外交上照例之客套語句，因採用此項文體之目的在備忘，故全文着重說明擬洽辦之事實與理由，使用時係負責交涉或洽辦人親帶面交對方者，文末多不簽名，亦不須 INITIAL，更不須蓋章。比如大公使奉本國政府電令，赴駐在國外交部洽商某事，使節多事先準備一備忘錄，將擬洽商事件，理由經過等用書面寫下，持交對方。

例　　一

駐美英大使爲建議向日政府採取一致行動事致國務院備忘錄

AIDE-MEMOIRE

The British Ambassador at Tokyo has been instructed to concert with his United States colleague and, provided he sees no serious objection, to call on the Japanese Minister for Foreign Affairs and, after conveying to him the information summarized in the annexure hereto and based on reports received from the British Consul General at Haiphong, to say that His Majesty's Government in the United Kingdom cannot but be gravely disquieted by the news that an ultimatum should have been delivered to the French authorities in Indo-China by the Japanese authorities on the spot without the knowledge and therefore presumably the consent of the Japanese Government. Sir Robert Craigie would add that His Majesty's Government find it difficult to escape the impression that advantage is being taken of the difficulties in which France and Indo-China find themselves to put pressure upon them to

agree to measures of profound political and strategic importance affecting not only Indo–China and China proper but all
countries who have interests in the Far East. In so far as
these measures appear to be designed to facilitate an attack
from a new quarter on the forces of the Chinese National
Government Sir Robert Craigie would add that they seem to
His Majesty's Government to be inconsistent with the spirit
of the Burma Road agreement. Finally Sir Robert Craigie
would express the hope that the Japanese Minister for Foreign
Affairs will be able to give him a reassuring reply to convey
to His Majesty's Government.

His Majesty's Government will be glad to know whether
the United States Government are prepared to instruct the
United States Ambassador at Tokyo to make further representations to the Japanese Government on lines similar to the
foregoing.

Washington, September……1940.

復　文
美國務院復英國大使館備忘錄

Aide–Mémoire

Reference is made to the British Embassy's Aide–Mémoire
of September…………1940 in which is expressed the desire of
the British Government to be informed whether the Government
of the United States would be prepared to instruct its Ambassador at Tokyo to make further representations to the Japanese
Government in regard to the situation in Indo–China.

Sir Robert Craigie was so kind as to make known to

Ambassador Grew the substance of the British Government's instructions as outlined in the Aide-Mémoire under reference. Sir Robert also made known the doubt, which it is understood he has expressed to his Government, whether further representations to the Japanese Government in regard to the subject under consideration would have a useful effect and the opinion that if such an approach should be made it would be inadvisable to refer to the Burma Road agreement.

In the light of the foregoing, the British Embassy may care to inform the Department of State whether the observations made by Sir Robert have caused the British Government to alter its view that further representations to the Japanese Government in regard to the situation in Into–China should be made at this time.

Washington, September ·········· 1940.

例　　二

Reference is made to the British Embassy's Aide-Mémoire of ··········, in regard to the situation in Thailand and French Indo-China.

The situation under reference has had the careful and continuing thought of the Government of the United States. This Government shares the view of the British Government that it would be desirable that the dispute between Thailand and French Indo-China be settled peacefully and without delay.

In the view of this Government, both Thailand and French Indo-China are in positions of insecurity. In both Thailand and French Indo-China there is division of counsel and of

— 21 —

attitude. As an inescapable background of the present situation in French Indo–China there is the fact of the defeat of France by an aggressive Germany. As an inescapable background of the present situation in Thailand there is the fact that a military minded Japan is embarked upon a course of aggression in the Far Eastern area. Given these backgrounds the permanence of any settlement that might be achieved in the near future would be doubtful and the adequacy of any guarantees that might be forthcoming would be questionable.

The Government of the United States recognizes the value of endeavor by diplomatic processes to influence the course of events in directions consistent with this Government's principles and objectives. This Government concurs in the view of the British Government that a proposal of open mediation by the United States and the British Government would be unlikely to succeed. In view of this belief and taking into account the situation, under reference against the background above described, this Government does not perceive what useful contribution along the lines of mediation it could make at the present time. Should negotiations between the two parties be undertaken directly or otherwise and should a situation develop in which the parties might consider that this Government could to advantage offer friendly counsel, this Government would, of course, be prepared to consider such proposal in the light of the attendant circumstances.

Washington, ············ 1941.

例　　　三

第二次大戰時中國政府為計劃派兵赴越事特發表備忘錄

In resisting Japanese aggression it has never been the intention of China to cause any troops to enter any foreign country provided Japanese forces do not in any way make use of its territory against China, any will not be ordered to march across the border as long as Japanese troops do not appear in Indo-China. It has now, however, been learned that Japan is planning to land troops in Indo-China and take other kinds of military action in the French colony with a view to attacking Chinese territory. The Government wishes to declare emphatically that in the event of actual entry of Japanese armed forces in Indo-China, under whatever pretext and under whatever conditions, the Chinese Government will consider it a direct and immediate menace to the security of China's territory, and will at once adopt measures of self-defense by despatching likewise armed forces to Indo-China to deal with the situation. The Chinese Government will be thus absolved from any responsibility for any consequences resulting from the adopting of such necessary measures. On the other hand, should the French authorities permit or tolerate any Japanese military activities in Indo-China, the French Government should not evade responsibility for all consequences, including any loss or damage that might be caused to the life and property of Chinese residents of Indo-China.

中國政府爲日本製造"滿州國"事件致九國公約簽字各國備忘錄

The Chinese Government has the honour to invite the attention of the ………… Government to the serious situation precipitated by Japan's announcement, on September 15, 1932, of her recognition of the so–called Manchukuo, an organization created, maintained and controlled by Japan in the Three Eastern Provinces of the Chinese Republic and by the publication of what purports to be a treaty between Japan and her puppet organization, whereby Japan may station troops in these Provinces at her free will and thus attempts to establish a virtual protectorate over that part of China's territory. This latest act of aggression on the part of Japan adds almost damaging link to the chain of international delinquencies perpetrated by her during the last twelve months, which consist not only in the usurpation of China's sovereign rights but in a continuous violation of international treaties of a most important character, including the Nine – Power Treaty concluded at Washington in 1923, to which ……………… is a signatory (an adherent) party.

It need not be recounted how Japan started her march of invasion on September 18, 1931, how she has since extended her military operations over a territory inhabited by 30,000,000 Chinese citizens, and how she has used sheer force in usurping the administrative powers of the Chinese Government and estabilishing a bogus administration in the area she has unlawfully occupied. All such facts are but too well–known to need recapitulation. Suffice it to say that from September 18, 1931, when Japanese troops opened their premeditated attack on Shenyang (Mukden) until the present time, not a day has passed without Japan aggravating her wrong by one act or another. The series of crimes of which Japan is guilty have now culminated in her recognition of the so-called Manchukuo.

Japan has attempted to deceive the world by advancing the ridiculous argument that the so-called Manchukuo was brought into existence by Chinese citizens who desired to secede from the Chinese Republic. Undeniable facts show that the bogus government in Manchuria is a product and a tool of Japanese Military aggression, pure and simple. A great number of Japanese who are directly responsible to the Government at Tokyo are dictating matters to the puppet organization, while the masses in Manchuria are under the constant oppression and intimidation of Japanese militarists. When the Japanese troops are withdrawn from Manchuria, the so-called Manchukuo would vanish completely.

By Article I of the Nine-Power Treaty, the Contracting Powers, other than China, agree, inter alia, to respect the sovereignty, the independence, and the territorial and administrative integrity of China. There is not the slightest doubt that Japan's recognition of her own puppet organization and all her previous actions so methodically performed in pursuance of her policy of aggression in Manchuria constitute a direct violation of China's sovereignty as well as her territorial and administrative integrity. It was with a view to preventing such a state of affairs as has now been brought about by Japan that the Powers entered into the engagements above referred to.

Japan is now not only victimizing China, but deliberately defies world opinion and sets at naught the solemn obligations she owes to other Powers. It cannot be conceived that Japan's actions should be permitted to go unchallenged and that the Nine-Power Treaty should be treated by those Powers which have subscribed to its engagements as a mere scrap of paper. The principle of the sanctity and inviolability of international treaties is at stake. When about 400,000 square miles of the territory of the Chinese Republic has been seized by Japanese military forces and when Japan has given her official sanction, against the advice and admonitions of friendly Powers, to the unlawful organization she has created in that territory, the painful consequences are not confined to China alone, but the peace of the world is ominously heartened.

In view of these circumstances, the Chinese Government considers that a grave situation has arisen which involves the application of stipulations of the Nine-Power Treaty and therefore, in accordance with Article 7 thereof, communicates its full and frank views to the Governments of those Powers which are parties to that Treaty, with the request that such measures be taken as will properly and effectively deal with the state of affairs brought about by Japan's acts of aggression in China, beginning with the attack on Shenyang (Mukden) on September 18, 1931, and culminating in the recognition of her puppet organization on September 15, 1932.

Nanking, September 16, 1932.

例　　五

1945 年柏林會議中美代表爲中國問題發表備忘錄

The Character and Scope of ·········· 's recent conversations in Moscow are of vital and immediate concern to us. They concern directly and may affect adversely our traditional and present policies and objectives with regard to China; e.g., observance of the "open door" and equality of opportunity; respect for the territorial and administrative integrity of China; and opposition to the growth of political and economic spheres of influence.

These policies are derived from and based firmly upon our national interest, more clearly now than at any time in the past. We are at war with Japan in defense of the principles underlying these policies.

We have, through our numerous missionary, social and cultural organizations, formed ties with China which are broad and deep. In the years just prior to the depression of 1929 Americans contributed about 60 million dollars annually to the support of missionary work in China. The attitude of these Americans, which is strongly "pro-Chinese", must be accorded consideration in our thinking and planning with regard to China.

When we first established treaty relations with China over one hundred years ago, we assumed the lead in obtaining "most favored nation" treatment with a view to protecting our merchants from discrimination. Since then, we have insisted upon equality of commercial opportunity for American nationals, with success except in areas of special interest (Russia and Japan in Manchuria). Just prior to Sino–Japanese hostilities (1937) we held first place in China's foreign trade.

Throughout this hundred year period, but more especially subsequent to the Spanish–American War, we have been aware that China under foreign domination or divided into spheres of foreign influence would threaten not only our commercial interests but also our security in the Pacific. The underlying cause of our involvement in war with Japan was our refusal to accept Japanese domination in China.

There is inherent in the settlements discussed by············ in Moscow a threat to our national interests in China and also to international cooperation to secure peace in the Pacific. This threat comes not from the actual language of the suggested settlements but from the potentialities of those settlements for future misapplication and friction.

Let us face the issue squarely with ourselves and with the Russians. The suggested settlements are in the main retrogressive. They are an expedient. They are not essential to general security in the Far East or to Russian security and they are not of a character to promote general participation in the economic development in China, including Manchuria. On the contrary they would lay the foundation for a sphere of political and economic interest. Irrespective of what disavowals may be made, they would constitute an infringement upon Chinese sovereignty and as such would be contrary to our policies and interests.

Berlin Conference, ············ 1945.

二、承認新國家與新政府

Recognition

國家形成之要素,一需要有固定之領土,一爲有一羣經營共同生活之人民,一爲有中央政府之組織,一爲具有獨立之主權,並能與他國發生外交關係。國際法對新國家之名稱,政體與政府之組織等向不過問,但問此政府有無能力,同時願否對外擔承國際義務,此點尤爲今日一般國際政治家特別注意。

政府爲國家執行政策之工具,代表國家行使統治權,因種種原因常有變動,甚至革命後發生政體變更,凡此皆須各既存政府予以承認,既存政府予以承認即表示承認之國家準備與被承認之國家隨時發生正式關係。因承認乃一國際行爲,爲已經存在之國家承認新成立國家具有國際法人之資格,可以參加國際社會,而成爲此社會之一份子。此新國家經承認後得享受國際間種種權利,同時亦須負擔國際間之種種義務。

承認之方式不一,有先予以事實承認 DE FACTO RECOGNI-TION 而繼以法律承認 DE JURE RECOGNITION 者,所謂事實承認即在種種行爲上承認對方國之政府所行爲之事實。構成此種事實之行爲,即足以代表正式或普通合法政府之行爲,如承認並接受新政府之代表,如與新政府之代表談判商約等。事實承認爲不確定的,爲有限度的。法律承認爲永久的,確定的,承認後可與被承認之國家建立外交關係,互換使節,有附條件予以承認者,如謂新政府須獲得全民投票贊成後始能予以承認,或新政府須負擔某項義務或清償某項債務後,始能獲得承認者。有各政府聯合行動者,有單獨行動者。

例　一

一九一九年美國務卿 LANSING 奉美總統之命行文波蘭臨時政府正式予以承認。

The President of the United States directs me to extend to you as Prime Minister and Secretary for Foreign Affairs of the Provisional Polish Government his sincere wishes for your success in the high office which you have assumed and his earnest hope that the Government of which you are a part will bring prosperity to the Republic of Poland.

It is my privilege to extend to you at this time my personal greetings and officially to assure you that it will be a source of gratification to enter into official relations with you at the earliest opportunity. To render to your country such aid as is possible at this time as it enters upon a new cycle of independent life, will be in full accord with that spirit of friendliness which has in the past animated the American people in their relations with your countrymen.

To the Foreign Minister

of the Iraqi Government

I am pleased to inform Your Excellency that the Council of Ministers of Greece has decided to recognize the new Government of Iraq.

In taking such action the Greek Government was prompted by the assurances publicly offered by the Iraqi Government to the effect that it will uphold Iraq's obligations under the international law and more especially those concerning the lawful rights and interests of foreigners in Iraq among whom scores of Greek nationals living and doing useful work in your country.

I feel also sure that the new Iraqi Government will do its best to contribute to the establishment of peace and stability in the Middle East with a view to the orderly advancement of all countries and peoples in that area for their own benefit and for the benefit of the whole world.

It is in that friendly spirit generally professed in Greece toward all members of the greater Arab family that I beg Your Excellency to convey to the Government and the people of Iraq the hearty wishes of the Greek Government and the Greek nation for best success and prosperity.

Greek Foreign Minister

例　　三

一九二六年美駐厄瓜多爾公使奉命通知厄政府美政府從即日起正式予以承認。

I have the honor to inform Your Excellency that I have been given instructions to say that the progress made by the Republic of Ecuador during the past three years since the *coup d'état* of July 9, 1925, and the tranquillity prevailing in Ecuador during that period, have been observed by my Government with a great deal of satisfaction. Having full confidence that the Government of Dr. Ayora has the support of the majority of the people of Ecuador, and is both capable and desirous of maintaining an orderly internal administration, and of observing with scrupulous care all international obligations, my Government is pleased to extend to it as from this date full recognition as the *de jure* Government of Ecuador.

例　　四

The United States government has received offcial notification of the establishment of the government of the Republic of Sudan and assurances from that government that it intends to honor its international obligations. The United States government has today been pleased to extend recognition to the government of Sudan with the expression of its best wishes.

三、開設使舘與徵求同意

Opening of Missions and Requesting for Agrément of Diplomatic Representatives

凡兩國政府有意建立外交關係，並派使在彼此首都駐紮，照例須於事先經過適當途徑洽商後，再由一方備文正式徵求對方同意，對方再復文表示接受，此項原則同意後，雙方即可選派使節。選派後再向對方政府徵求對此項人選能否接受之同意（法文稱 agrément），如對方政府決定接受，應用書面答復，或用其他適當方式表示同意，派遣政府接到同意答復後始可發表。

以上係就兩國向無外交關係新設駐使而言，如兩國向有邦交，亦有使節派駐對方國首都，欲更換使節（或因舊使節奉令他調，或因任期屆滿，或因年老退休或其他原因必須離職），亦應經過上述徵求對擬派新使同意之手續，始能對外發表。

一國派遣新使，在未獲得對方國政府同意以前，絕不宜發表，因恐對方拒絕接受而發生尷尬現象，此項拒絕接受之事例在各國外交史中屢見不鮮。

拒絕接受之情形與理由甚多，有因擬被任命之使節以往言論行為等對方國認為對其不利者，有因政治宗教原因者，在昔日宮廷之間，更有因婚姻以及帝王個人間之仇恨而考慮其對使節派遣之接受與否者。對方國政府拒絕接受使節之派遣可不必說明理由，派遣國亦不加深究，亦不得視此為不友好之行為，因為一個獨立主權國家自有全權決定接受或不接受另一國家之使節，事實上派遣一個不受歡迎之使節前往他國駐紮，自無法盼其促進邦交，達成使命，此本理之常，無待贅述。又在原則上一個國家僅能派遣使節一人駐紮某國，但一國使節可同時兼駐兩國或兩個以上之國家而不致引起反對。

本節所舉一、二、三各例，皆旨在建交設館，有復文者均附復文，四、五、六、七、八、九、十、十一十二各例乃選派使節徵求同意事例。本節最後兩篇，係關於開設領事館並派遣領事之文例。一國政府派駐新領事，到任後必須取得駐在國政府之憑證，此項證書乃駐在國政府對新領事之承認，即承認新領事有權行使其職權。關於本國政府發給之領事委任文憑，及駐在國政府頒發之領事證書格式等，請參閱本書後面"國書"一節。

例　　　一

....

Sir,

　At the instance of His Majesty's Government in the Commonwealth of Australia and under the instructions from His Majesty's principal Secretary of State for Foreign Affairs I have the honour to inform you that His Majesty's Government in the Commonwealth of Australia have come to the conclusion that it is desirable that the handling of matters in China relating to Australia should be confided to an Envoy Extraordinary and Minister Plenipotentiary.

　Such a Minister would be accredited by His Majesty The King to the Chairman of the National Government of the Republic of China and he would be furnished with credentials which would enable him to take charge of all affairs relating to Australia. He would be the ordinary channel of communication with the Chinese Government on these matters. The arrangements proposed would not denote any departure from the principle of the diplomatic unity of the Empire, that is to say, the principle of consultation and cooperation among His Majesty's Representatives as among His Majesty's Governments themselves in matters of Common concern. The method of dealing with matters which may arise concerning more than one of the Governments would therefore be settled by consultation between the representatives of the Governments concerned.

In proposing the establishment of an Australian Legation His Majesty's Government in the Commonwealth of Australia trust that it will promote the maintenance and development of cordial relations not only between China and Australia but also between China and the whole of the British Commonwealth of Nations.

I avail myself of this opportunity to renew to your Excellency the assurance of my highest consideration.

(Signed) BRITISH AMBASSADOR

His Excellency

Dr. ·····················

Minister of Foreign Affairs

·····················

....

Sir,

I have the honour to acknowledge the receipt of Your Excellency's note of·········· proposing the establishment of an Australian Legation in China with an Envoy Extraordinary and Minister Plenipotentiary as its head.

In reply, I have the honour to state that the Chinese Government gladly accepts the proposal and has decided to send an Envoy Extraordinary and Minister Plenipotentiary to Australia in the immediate future.

I have the honour to add that the Chinese Government shares the hope expressed by His Majesty's Government in the Commonwealth of Australia that the proposed exchange of diplomatic missions will promote the maintenance and development of cordial relations not only between China and Australia but also between China and the whole of the British Commonwealth of Nations.

I avail myself of this opportunity to renew to Your Excellency the assurance of my highest consideration.

(Signed) CHINESE FOREIGN MINISTER

His Excellency
    Sir ····················,
    His Britannic Majesty's Ambassador to China
    ····················

復　　文

....

Sir,

With reference to my note to Your Excellency's predecessor dated May 28th last and to Dr. Wang Chung-hui's reply of the 3rd June regarding the appointment of an Australian Minister to China, I have the honour to inform you that His Majesty's Government in the Commonwealth of Australia propose to appoint the Honourable Sir ....to fill this post.

I should be glad to learn whether this appointment would. be acceptable to the Chinese Government.

I avail myself of this opportunity to renew to Your Excellency the assurance of my highest consideration,

(signed) BRITISH AMBASSADOR

His Excellency

　　Dr. ....,

　　Minister of Foreign Affairs,

　　　　....................

例 二

Excellency,

Under instructions from my Government, I have the honour to propose to Your Excellency the establishment of diplomatic relations between our two countries, and to convey the intention of my Government to set up an Embassy in...... in the immediate future.

Please accept, Your Excellency, the assurances of my highest consideration.

Ambassador Extraordinary and
Plenipotentiary of the Republic
of China to.............

His Excellency

    Mr.....................

    Minister of Foreign Affairs of

      the Republic of...........

      ....

復　文

Excellency,

I have the honour to acknowledge receipt of your letter of ...., conveying your Government's proposal for estabishing diplomatic relations between the Republic of......... and the Republic of .... and its intention to set up an Embassy in .... in the immediate future.

In reply I have pleasure in informing Your Excellency that the Government of the Republic of .... welcomes the proposal of your Government and its intention to set up an Embassy in .... and wishes to assure that it looks forward to cordial and friendly relations between the two countries.

Please accept, Your Excellency, the assurances of my highest conideration.

....

Minister of Foreign Affairs

of the Republic of ....

His Excellency Mr. ....

Ambassador Extraordinary and Plenipotentiary

of the Republic of China to ....

例 三

JOINT COMMUNIQUE

The Government of the Islamic Republic of Mauritania and the Government of the Republic of China, desirous of developing a close mutual cooperation and strengthening the friendly ties between the peoples of the two republics, have decided to establish diplomatic relations between the two countries. To this purpose the Government of the Islamic Republic of Mauritania agrees to the opening at Nouakchott of the Embassy of the Republic of China.

例 四

政府選派使節徵求對方國政府之同意。

Excellency:

On instructions of my Government, I have the honor to inform Your Excellency that my Government intends to recall me for reassignment and to appoint Dr. ············ to the post of Ambassador Extraordinary and Plenipotentiary of the Republic of China to the Republic of ····················

In submitting herewith to Your Excellency the *curriculum vitae* of Dr. ············, I am instructed to seek the agrément of Your Excellency's Government to Dr. ·············'s appointment.

Accept, Excellency, the renewed assurances of my highest consideration.

(SGD.) ················

例　　　五

Sir,

I have the honour to inform you that the National Government of the Republic of China proposes to appoint Dr. Vi Kyuin Wellington Koo as Ambassador Extraordinary and Plenipotentiary to the Court of St. James, and I am instructed by my Government to enquire as to whether His Majesty's Government will regard the proposal as acceptable.

I avail myself of this opportunity to renew to Your Excellency the assurance of my highest consideration.

(signed) ··················

His Excellency
　Lord ················
　　Secretary for Foreign Affairs
　　London

復　　　文

FOREIGN OFFICE, S.W.I.

....

Sir,

In his note No. F.C. 41/33 of the 16th April Dr. Quo Tai-chi was good enough to enquire whether His Majesty's Government would regard as acceptable the proposal of the National Government of the Republic of China to appoint Dr. Vi Kyuin Wellington Koo as Ambassador Extraordinary and Plenipotentiary of China at this Court.

In reply I have pleasure in informing you that the appointment of Dr. Wellington Koo in the capacity mentioned is agreeable to the King.

I have the honour to be, with high consideration,

Sir,

Your obedient servant,
(for the Secretary of State)
(signed)··························

Dr. ·····················

Counsellor of the Chinese Embassy
LONDON

例　　六

Mr. Chargé d'Affaires,

Acting under special instructions from my Government, I have the honour to request you to convey to your Government that my Government, wishing to strengthen still more the friendly ties already existing between our two countries, has decided to appoint Mr. ············ as Ambassador Extraordinary and Plenipotentiary to the Republic of ············

It will naturally be much appreciated if the agreement of your Government to such an appointment can be given and transmitted to me as soon as possible.

Mr. ············ has had, in many capacities, a distinguished career. I am enclosing two copies of his *curriculum vitae* for the information of your Government.

Please accept, Mr. Chargé d'Affaires, the assurance of my distinguished consideration.

Mr. ·····················,

Chargé d'Affaires,

Embassy of the Republic of ············

·····················

Excellency:

I have the honor to inform Your Excellency that the state of Ambassador ·················'s health will not permit him to continue as United States Ambassador to the Republic of······.

I also have the honor, under instructions from my Government, to request the agrément of the Government of the Republic of ············· to the appointment of ················ as Ambassador Extraordinary and Plenipotentiary to ··············. The attached sheet contains brief biographic data on ············.

Accept, Excellency, the renewed assurances of my highest consideration.

(Signed)·····················

Exclosure:

Biographic Data Sheet

H.E.

······················

······················

復　　文
中國外交部部長復○國臨時代辦照會

關於

貴國政府擬任命…………爲…………駐華特命全權大使徵求同意事，
貴代辦本年○月○日照會敬悉。

本部長茲奉告

貴代辦：中華民國政府對於…………政府任命…………爲駐華特命全
權大使一節，欣表同意；並對…………大使因病不克返任一節，深表
惋惜，請惠予轉達　貴國政府爲荷。

本部長順向

貴代辦申致本人崇高之敬意

此致

…………駐華臨時代辦…………先生

…………………（簽名）

中華民國○○年○月○日　於臺北

例　　八

關於…………共和國擬任命…………先生爲駐華特命全權大使徵
求中華民國政府同意事。

貴大使與本部…………政務次長…………談話暨…………先生簡歷均
敬悉。

本部長茲特奉告

貴大使，中華民國政府對於…………共和國擬任命…………先生爲駐
華特命全權大使一節，欣表同意，請惠予轉達

貴國政府。本部長並對　閣下離華深表惜別之意。

本部長順向

貴大使申致最崇高之敬意。

此致

…………共和國駐華特命全權大使…………閣下

外交部部長…………（簽名）

例　九

關於…………政府擬任命…………先生爲駐中華民國特命全權大使事。

貴代辦……月……日來照業經閱悉。中華民國政府對…………先生之任命，敬表同意。相應照復，即希

查照轉達爲荷。

本部長順向

貴代辦重表敬意。

　　　此致

…………共和國駐華大使館臨時代辦…………先生

　　　　　　　　外交部部長…………（簽名）

例　十

接准

貴大使……月……日照會略開：貴大使奉令回國，…………政府擬任命…………繼任駐中華民國特命全權大使，徵求中國政府同意等由；本政務次長代理部務茲代表中國政府表示同意。

本政務次長代理部務順向

貴大使重表最崇高之敬意。

　　　此致

…………國駐中華民國特命全權大使…………閣下

　　　　　　　政務次長代理部務…………（簽名）

例 十 一

NOTE VERBALE

Le Ministère Royal des Affaires Etrangères présente ses compliments à l'Ambassade de ·············· à ·············· et a l'honneur de porter à sa cannaissance que le Gouvernement ············ désire accréditer Son Excellence Monsieur ············ auprès du Gouvernement de ············, en qualité d'Ambassadeur et prie que l'agrément d'usage lui soit accordé.

Ce Département Royal saisit cette occasion pour renouveler à l'Ambassade de ····················· les assurances de sa haute considération.

·····················

復 文

NOTE VERBALE

L'Ambassade de présente ses compliments au Ministère Royal des Affaires Etrangères et en réponse à Sa Note No. ············ du 25 Novembre. a l'honneur de porter à sa connaissance que le Gouvernement de la République de ·············· a accordé son agrément pour la nomination de Son Excellence Monsieur ············ en qualité d'Ambassadeur.

Le Gouvernement de la République de ············ a exprimé le désir que la nomination de Son Excellence ·············· soit annoncée en même temps à ·············· et à ·············· Cette Ambassade saurait donc gré au dit Ministère de bien vouloir lui communiquer quelle serait la date qui conviendrait le mieux à ce Ministère pour l'annonce en question.

L'Ambassade de ····················· saisit cette occasion pour renouveler au Ministère Royal des Affaires Etrangères les assurances de sa très haute considération.

·····················

Sur les instructions de son Gouvernement, la Légation de Chine a l'honneur de porter à la connaissance de l'honorable Ministère des Affaires Etrangères de la République Turque que son Gouvernement a l'intention de nommer Monsieur le Dr. ...., Membre de l'Assemblée Consultative et professeur de l'Université Fédérale du Sud–Ouest en Chine, comme Envoyé Extraordinaire et Ministre Plénipotentiaire de Chine auprès du Gouvernement de la République Turque.

Cette Légation est très obligée au Ministère de vouloir bien faire des démarches nécéssaires auprès de son Gouvernement pour qu'Il lui accorde Son agrément.

Ankara, le·······················

······················

復 文

Le Ministère des Affaires Etrangères a l'honneur d'informer la Légation de la République Chinoise, en réponse à Sa Note No. ········ du ········ que le Gouvernement de la République accorde avec plaisir son agrément à la nomination de Monsieur le Docteur ··············· en qualité d'Envoyé Extraordinaire et Ministre Plénipotentiaire de Chine en Turquie.

Ankara, le·······················

A la Légation de la République Chinoise
Ankara

例　十　三

關於開設領館派駐領事之文件。

Monsieur le Ministre,

Sur les instructions de mon Gouvernement, j'ai l'honneur de porter à la connaissance de Votre Excellence que le Gouvernement ………… a décidé d'établir un Consulat de ………… à …………

Monsieur …………, Premier Secrétaire de cette Ambassade, a été transféré de son poste actuel et nommé Consul de……… à …………

Avant l'arrivée des Lettres de Provision pour réquérir l'Exéquatur, j'ai l'honneur de prier Votre Excellence de vouloir bien accorder à Monsieur ………… reconnaissance provisoire afin que ce dernier puisse assumer dès maintenant ses fonctions consulaires.

Veuillez agréer, Monsieur le Ministre, les assurances de ma plus haute considération.

(SGD.) …………………

Son Excellence

　　Monsieur …………………

　　Ministre des Affaires Etrangères

　　　　…………………

例　十　四

Note Verbale.

The American Embassy, acting under instructions from its Government, has the honor to inform the Imperial Ministry for Foreign Affairs that Mr. ⋯⋯⋯has been appointed Consul of the United States of America at Bremen, as appears from the accompanying commission, and to request that the Imperial Government will kindly cause the necessary steps to be taken towards the formal recognition of Mr. ⋯⋯⋯⋯ in the above capacity.

Date.

To the

Imperial Foreign Office.

四、到 任

Arrival at Post

新使節到任，首先須約期晋見駐在國外交部部長，當面遞交到任國書副本及呈遞國書所擬致頌詞副本。關於請見元首呈遞到任國書日期，可在謁見外交部長時面請，或另備函洽請（見本節例一，例二及例三）。

在未向駐在國元首正式呈遞到任國書前，新使節不公開對外活動，亦不拜訪駐在同一首都之他國使節。此處所謂"不公開對外活動"，即指不以新使節名義正式對外參加拜訪應酬集會等活動。如果新任使節願拜訪駐在地之外交團領袖大使（英文 Dean of the Diplomatic Corps 或法文 Doyen du Corps Diplomatique），先取得聯繫，並探詢有關呈遞國書典禮事宜，駐在國政府一般習慣及外交團種種，該領袖大使自亦表歡迎，如其他駐使中有熟識者或經人介紹相識者，亦可非正式拜訪。

呈遞國書後應即通知各國使節，通知文件用正式照會格式，由新使節親自簽名，不必再加蓋館印，文內措詞大意爲通知奉命擔任之職務全衒，告以到任國書業已向駐在國元首呈遞，希望與受文國家使節在公務與私交上維持友好關係，受文使節對上項來文多正式復文。如駐在國外交團之領袖大使所代表之國家與本國無邦交，仍可去文通知業已呈遞國書各節，但不必提及一般習用之增進兩使館間之友好關係一類詞語。（見本節第十八例，發文者爲阿拉伯聯合共和國之駐希臘大使，而兼任駐希外交團之領袖大使者爲中華民國駐希大使，該兩國在發文時無邦交，但爲外交團公務，仍可來往行文。）

如使館升格後，即由公使館升格爲大使館後，使節就任大使新職，可同時通知（見本節例九），亦可分別通知。

　　代辦分為兩種，　一種稱為永久或常駐代辦　CHARGE　D'AF-FAIRES *ad hoc* 或 CHARGE D'AFFAIRES *en titre* 或 TITULAR CHARGE D' AFFAIRES 或 CHARGE D'AFFAIRES *en pied*,種稱為臨時代辦 CHARGE D'AFFAIRES *ad interim* (或CHARGE D'AFFAIRES a.i.)，此處所論之代辦乃指前一種而言，習慣上常駐代辦僅稱 Chargé d'Affaires。其到任僅向駐在國外交部長呈遞代辦到任書，無向元首呈遞到任國書手續與典禮，故向外交部長呈遞到任書後，卽須備文通知同駐在地之其他使節（見本節例十及例十九），各使節接到此項通知後，在禮節上亦多備文答復（見本節例二十五）。

　　至各級館員到任，手續更為簡單，照例由服務之使館備文通知駐在國外交部及其他使館，說明姓名、職位及到任日期卽可，此種行文多用節略。

　　茲將所舉館長到任各例，分英文法文兩類列之，另一類為館長到任復文。最後將有關館員到任之文件另成一類。

舘長到任 (英文)

Chiefs of Mission

例　　　一

BRITISH EMBASSY
CHUNGKING
....

Sir,

I have the honour to inform Your Excellency that I have today requested to be informed of the date when it will please His Excellency the President of the National Government of China to receive me in audience for the purpose of presenting my Letters of Credence from His Majesty the King. I have the honour to enclose herein a list of the names in English and Chinese of the gentlemen who will accompany me on that occasion.

I avail myself of this opportunity to renew (convey) to Your Excellency the assurances of my highest consideration.

(signed) BRITISH AMBASSADOR

His Excellency

Doctor ······················

Minister for Foreign Affairs.

....

Excellency:

I have the honour to inform Your Excellency that the President of the United States of America having accredited me as Ambassador Extraordinary and Plenipotentiary to the Republic of China, I have now arrived in ·········· to take up my duties.

I should be grateful if Your Excellency would be so kind as to fix a convenient time when I may call on you to hand you a copy of my Letter of Credence and to request that the pleasure of His Excellency the Chairman of the National Government be ascertained for an audience for the formal presentation of my credentials.

Accept, Excellency, the assurances of my highest consideration.

(signed) AMERICAN AMBASSADOR

His Excellency

Dr. ·····················

Minister for Foreign Affairs

....

....

Excellency:

I have the honor to inform Your Excellency that, having been appointed by the President as Ambassador Extraordinary and Plenipotentiary to represent the United States of America near the person of His Majesty the Emperor and King, I have arrived at my post and assumed the direction of the Embassy.

I have, in consequence, the honor to request Your Excellency to kindly ascertain the convenience of Their Imperial and Royal Majesties and to inform me as to when I may be graciously accorded an opportunity of presenting to His Majesty the Emperor and King my Letters of Credence, and as to the pleasure of Her Majesty the Empress and Queen toward granting me the distinguished honor of an audience.

I embrace this opportunity to convey to Your Excellency the assurances of my highest consideration.

(Signed) ....

Enclosure: Office copy of Letters of Credence.
His Excellency.

`......................

Imperial Secretary of State for Foreign Affairs,
　　etc., 　　　　　etc., 　　　　　etc.

例　　四

Embassy of the

United States of America

……………………..

Excellency:

I have the honor to　inform Your Excellency that I have on this date presented my letter of credence to His Excellency the President of the Republic of the ……… and have assumed my duties as Ambassador Extraordinary and Plenipotentiary of the United States of America to the …………

I avail myself of this opportunity to express the assurances of my desire to continue the close and cordial relations which have always existed between our two Missions.

Please accept, Excellency, the assurances of my highest consideration.

(SGD.) AMERICAN AMBASSADOR

His Excellency

……………………,

Ambassador of the Republic of China,

…………………..

例　　五

Excellency,

　　I have the honour to inform you that I have today presented to His Excellency the President of the ·········· Republic
the Letters which accredit me as Ambassador Extraordinary
and Plenipotentiary of Canada in ···········

　　May I take this opportunity of saying that I look forward
with pleasure to the continuation of the good relations, both
personal and official, which exist between our two Missions
and which reflect the friendship between our two countries.

　　Please accept, Excellency, the assurances of my highest
consideration.

······················

例　　六

Excellency,

　　I have the honor to inform you that I have presented
today to His Majesty Paul J, King of the Hellenes, the Letters
accrediting me as Ambassador Extraordinary and Plenipotentiary of ··········· to Greece.

　　It gives me great pleasure thus to enter into official and
personal association with you and I take this opportunity to
express my earnest desire to maintain the cordial relations
existing between our respective missions.

　　Please accept, Excellency, the assurances of my highest
consideration.

(SGD.) ·····················

Excellency,

I have the honour to inform you that I have today presented Letters of Credence from the Provisional President of the Argentine Republic, His Excellency General ················,
to His Excellency President ··············, which accredit me as Envoy Extraordinary and Minister Plenipotentiary to the ········

I avail myself of the opportunity to express my sincere desire to strengthen and maintain the cordial and warm relations existent between our two Missions.

Accept, Excellency, the assurances of my high regard and consideration.

·····························

例　　八

Your Excellency,

I have the honour to inform Your Excellency that I have today presented to His Majesty King ············ of the ············,
the letter of my credentials by which the President of the Supreme Commission of the Republic of the ············ appoints me Envoy Extraordinary and Minister Plenipotentiary of the Republic of the ············ to the Kingdom of ············

On the assumption of my post, I sincerely express to you that it will be my endeavour to establish good relations, both official and personal, with you with a view to strengthening the friendly relations between our two countries.

I avail myself of this opportunity to express to you the assurance of my highest consideration.

·····························

Excellency,

I have the honor to inform Your Excellency that, effective ············, the Legation of the Republic of ··········· in ············ has been elevated to the status of an Embassy in accordance with the agreement arrived at between the authorities of the Republic of ············ and the Republic of the ············

I have the further honor to inform Your Excellency that I have today presented to His Excellency the President of the Republic of the ··············· the Letters of Credence from His Excellency the President of the Republic of ········ accrediting me as Ambassador Extraordinary and Plenipotentiary of········ to the ············

I avail myself of this opportunity to express the sincere desire to continue and enhance the close cooperation and friendly relations which exist between our two Missions.

Accept, Excellency, the renewed assurances of my highest consideration.

······························

Your Excellency,

I have the honour to inform you that I was today received by His Excellency the Minister of Foreign Affairs, on which occasion I presented to him the Letters which accredit me to the ············ Government in the capacity of Chargé d'Affaires of the ···············

Please accept, Your Excellency, the renewed assurance of my highest consideration.

(Signed)······················

舘長到任（法文）

....

Monsieur l'Ambassadeur,

J'ai l'honneur de faire connaître à Votre Excellence que j'ai remis aujourd'hui à S.E. Monsieur le Président de la République des ·········· les lettres de créance m'accréditant en qualité d'Ambassadeur Extraordinaire et Plénipotentiaire de la République Française.

Avant même d'avoir l'honneur de rendre visite à Votre Excellence, je tiens à l'assurer de mon·vif désir d'entretenir et de resserrer les cordiales relations qui ont toujours existé entre nos deux missions.

Je prie Votre Excellence de bien vouloir agréer les assurances de ma très haute considération.

Son Excellence

Monsieur·····················

Ambassadeur Extraordinaire et

Plénipotentiaire de Chine

....

例 十 二

Monsieur l'Ambassadeur,

J'ai l'honneur de porter à la connaissance de Votre Excellence que j'ai été admis aujourd'hui a présenter à Son Excellence le Président de la République ·········· les Lettres qui m'accréditent auprès de Lui en qualité d'Ambassadeur Extraordinaire et Plénipotentiaire de ······················.

Je me félicite de cette occasion qui me permet d'entrer en rapports tant officiels que personnels avec Votre Excellence et je La prie de croire que tous mes efforts tendront à maintenir les excellentes relations qui existent, si heureusement, entre nos deux Missions.

Veuillez agréer, Monsieur l'Ambassadeur, les assurances de ma trés haute considération.

······························

例 十 三

Monsieur l'Ambassadeur,

J'ai l'honneur de porter à la connaissance de Votre Excellence que j'ai remis aujourd'hui entre les mains de Sa Majesté le Roi des ·········· les Lettres qui m'accréditent auprès de Lui en qualité d'Ambassadeur Extraordinaire et Plénipotentiaire de la République du Liban.

En me félicitant de l'occasion qui m'est ainsi offerte d'entrer en relations tant officielles que personnelles avec Votre Excellence, je tiens à l'assurer que je ne négligerai rien pour les rendre conformes aux excellents rapports qui existent si heureusement entre nos deux Pays.

Veuillez agréer, Monsieur l'Ambassadeur, les assurances de ma très haute considération.

(Ambassadeur de Liban)

Monsieur l'Ambassadeur,

J'ai l'honneur de porter à la connaissance de Votre Excellance que j'ai remis aujourd'hur entre les mains de Sa Majesté le Roi des ··········· les Lettres qui m'accréditent auprès d'Elle en qualité d'Ambassadeur Extraordinaire et Plénipotentiaire du

··················

En me félicitant de l'occasion qui m'est ainsi donnée d'entrer en relations tant officielles que personnelles avec Votre Excellence, je tiens à L'assurer que je ne négligerai rien pour les rendre conformes aux excellents rapports qui existent si heureusement entre nos deux Pays.

Veuillez agréer, Monsieur l'Ambassadeur, les assurances de ma très haute considération.

··························

Son Excellence le Dr.··············

　Ambassadeur Extraordinaire et

　　Plénipotentiaire de ··············

　　En Ville.

Monsieur l'Ambassadeur'

J'ai l'honneur de porter à la connaissance de Votre Excellence que j'ai été admis aujourd'hui a présenter à Son Excellence Monsieur ···········, Président de la République ···········, les Lettres qui m'accréditent auprès de Lui en qualité d'Ambassadeur Extraordinaire et Plénipotentiaire du···········

Je serais heureux de pouvoir entretenir avec Votre Excellance les meilleurs rapports officiels et personnels et je Le prie de croire que je ne négligerai rien pour rendre conformes en tout, les bonnes relations qui existent si heureusement entre nos deux Missions.

Je serais reconnaissant à Votre Excellence, si Elle voudrait bien me faciliter dans l'accomplissement de mon devoir.

Veuillez agréer, Monsieur l'Ambassadeur, les assurances de ma plus haute considération.

....

例 十 六

Excellence,

J'ai l'honneur d'informer Votre Excellence que j'ai présenté aujourd'hui à Son Excellence Monsieur le Président de la République des ············ les lettres par lesquelles Sa Majesté ············ m'accrédite comme Envoyé Extraordinaire et Ministre Plénipotentiaire du Royaume du ············ auprès du Gouvernement de la République des ········, avec résidence à Bangkok (Ambassade Royale du ············ à Bangkok).

Je saisis cette occasion pour présenter mes compliments à Votre Excellence et lui exprimer l'espoir que j'entretiens de voir s'établir entre nos deux missions tant sur le plan officiel que personnel, les relations les plus cordiales.

Je vous prie d'agréer, Excellence, les assurances de ma plus haute considération.

....

Son Excellence Monsieur ············
  Ambassador
   Extraordinary and Plenipotentiary
    of the Republic of ············

例 十 七

Monsieur l'Ambassadeur,

J'ai l'honneur, Excellence, d'accuser réception de Votre lettre du ············, par laquelle Vous avez bien voulu me faire savoir que Vous avez presenté le même jour, à Son Excellence Monsieur ············, Président de la République ············, les Lettres qui Vous accréditent auprès de Lui en qualité d'Ambassadeur Extraordinaire et Plénipotentiaire du ············

Je Vous remercie, Monsieur l'Ambassadeur, de cette obligeante communication et je tiens à mon tour à exprimer la satisfaction que j'éprouve à entretenir les meilleurs rapports officieles et personnels avec Votre Excellence. Je Vous prie de croire également, que je ne négligerai rien pour rendre conformes en tout, les bonnes relations qui existent si heureusement entre nos deux Missions.

Veuillez agréer, Monsieur l'Ambassadeur, les assurances de ma plus haute considération.

例 十 八

Excellence,

J'ai l'honneur de porter à la connaissance de Votre Excellence que j'ai remis aujourd'hui entre les mains de Sa Majesté Paul ler, Roi des Hellénes, les Lettres qui m'accréditent auprès de Lui en qualité d'Ambassadeur Extraordinaire et Plénipotentiaire de la République Arabe Unie.

Je Vous prie d'agréer, Excellence, les assurances de ma très haute considération.

AMBASSADEUR DE R.A.U.

Son Excellence
   Monsieur le Doyen du
    Corps Diplomatique,
    EN VILLE.

例 十 九

Monsieur l'Ambassadeur,

J'ai l'honneur d'informer Votre Excellence qu'en date d'aujourd'hui j'ai présenté à Son Excellence le Ministre des Affaires Extrangères les Lettres de Cabinet qui m'accréditent comme Chargé d'Affaires du ·········· auprès du Gouvernement ············.

En cette circonstance j'ai le plaisir d'exprimer à Votre Excellence mon sincère désir d'établir les relations les plus cordiales, aussi bien officielles que personnelles, avec Votre Excellence afin de contribuer ainsi à resserrer les liens d'amitié qui unissent nos deux pays.

Je profite de cette opportunité pour présenter à Votre Excellence l'assurance de ma considération la plus haute et distinguée.

······························

A Son Excellence··················

Ambassadeur Extraordinaire

et Plénipotentiaire de ············.

···················

舘長到任復文

Replies

例 二 十

Monsieur l'Ambassadeur,

J'ai l'honneur d'accuser réception à Votre Excellence de la lettre du ·········· par laquelle Vous avez bien voulu me faire savoir que Vous avez présenté le même jour à Son Excellence le Président de la République ···········, les Lettres qui Vous accréditent auprès de Lui en qualité d'Ambassadeur Extraordinaire et Plénipotentiaire de ············.

Je remercie Votre Excellence de cette obligeante communication et me félicite à mon tour de l'occasion qui m'est ainsi donnée d'entrer en rapports tant officiels que personnels avec Vous. Je tiens également à assurer Votre Excellence que tous mes efforts tendront à maintenir les excellentes relations qui existent si heureusement entre nos deux Missions.

Veuillez agréer, Monsieur l'Ambassadeur, les assurances de ma très haute considération.

····························

Son Excellence

Monsieur ···········

Ambassadeur Extraordinaire

et Plénipotentiaire de ············

············

例 二 十 一

Monsieur l'Ambassadeur,

J'ai l'honneur d'accuser réception de la lettre de Votre Excellence datée du 12 Décembre par laquelle Vous avez bien voulu porter à ma connaissance que Vous avez remis entre les mains de Sa Majesté le Roi des ·········· les Lettres qui Vous accréditent en qualité d'Ambassadeur Extraordinaire et Plénipotentiaire de la République Fédérale d'Allemagne.

Je me félicite de l'occasion qui m'est ainsi donnée d'entrer en relations tant officielles que personnelles avec Votre Excellence et tiens à Vous assurer que je ferai de mon mieux pour les rendre conformes aux excellents rapports qui existent entre nos deux missions.

Veuillez agréer, Monsieur l'Ambassadeur, les assurances de ma très haute considération.

(SGD.) Chinese Ambassador

Son Excellence

M. ·····················

Ambassadeur d'Allemagne

En Ville.

例 二 七 二

Monsieur l'Ambassadeur,

J'ai l'honneur d'accuser réception de la letter de Votre Excellence datée du 12 Octobre par laquelle Vous avez bien voulu porter à ma connaissance que Vous avez remis à Sa Majesté ··············, Roi des ··············, les Lettres qui Vous accréditent en qualité d'Ambassadeur Extraordinaire et Plénipotentiaire des Etats–Unis d'Amérique en ··············

Je me félicite de l'occasion qui m'est ainsi donnée d'entrer en relations officielles et personnelles avec Votre Excellence et Vous assure que je ferai tout mon possible pour les rendre conformes aux excellents rapports qui existent entre nos deux pays et Missions.

Veuillez agréer, Monsieur l'Ambassadeur, les assurances de ma très haute considération.

(Signature)

Son Excellence
Monsieur ············
Ambassadeur des Etats-Unis d'Amérique
En Ville.

例 二 十 三

·······················

Monsieur l'Ambassadeur,

Votre Excellence a bien voulu, par Sa lettre du ············ courant, me faire savoir qu'Elle a été admise à présenter à Sa Majesté, l'Empereur et Roi, les lettres qui L'accréditent auprès d'Elle en qualité d'Ambassadeur Extraordinaire et Plénipotentiaire de ············

I'ai l'honneur d'accuser réception à Votre Excellence de cette communication, et, en La remerciant des sentiments qu'Elle veut bien m'exprimer à cette occasion, je suis heureux de Lui dire que je suis aussi désireux qu'Elle de maintenir entre l'Ambassade de ················· et Celle des États-Unis d'Amérique, des relations conformes à celles qui existent si heureusement entre nos deux pays.

Veuilles agréer, Monsieur l'Ambassadeur, l'assurance de ma très haute considération.

(Signature)

Son Excellence,
Monsieur ············,
Ambassadeur de ············à Berlin.

例 二 十 四

如兩使館所代表之國家間暫無邦交，或邦交因事中斷，新任使節願去文對方通知到任各節，對方使館似亦不可不復文，但宜在措詞上避免提及兩國間友好關係一類詞語，見下例：

Excellency:

I have the honor to acknowledge the receipt of your note of ⋯⋯⋯⋯, informing me that Your Excellency has presented to His Excellency, the President of the Republic of the⋯⋯⋯⋯, Letters of Credence, accrediting you as Envoy Extraordinary and Minister Plenipotentiary of Switzerland in the ⋯⋯⋯⋯⋯

While appreciating your informing me personally of your assumption of duties as Envoy Extraordinary and Minister Plenipotentiary of Switzerland, I avail myself of this opportunity to reciprocate your desire to continue the cordial personal relations which so happily exist between us.

Accept, Excellency, the assurances of my highest consideration.

例 二 十 五

Monsieur le Chargé d'Affaires,

J'ai l'honneur d'accuser réception de votre lettre du ⋯⋯⋯ ⋯⋯ par laquelle vous avez bien voulu porter à ma connaissance que vous avez présenté à Son Excellence le Ministre des Affaires Etrangères les Lettres vous accréditant auprès du Gouvernement Royal ⋯⋯⋯⋯⋯ en qualité de Chargé d'Affaires de ⋯⋯⋯⋯⋯⋯⋯

En vous remerciant de cette obligeante communication

dont j'ai pris bonne note, je vous prie d'agréer, Monsieur le Chargé d'Affaires, les assurances de ma considération distinguée.

(Signed) Chinese Ambassador

Monsieur ···········
Chargé d'Affaires de ············
························
···········

舘 員 到 任
Staff Members of Mission

例 二 十 六

Her Britannic Majesty's Embassy present their compliments to the Diplomatic Missions in ··········· and have the honor to inform them that Air Commodore ···········, O.B.E., A.F.C., accompanied by his wife, arrived in ··········· on ···········, to join the staff of the Embassy.

On the 1st of February Air Commodore will assume duty as Air Attache at the Embassy in place of Air Commodore ···········, O. B.E., D.F.C., who will be leaving ··········· on the ··········· on transfer.

Her Britannic Majesty's Embassy avail themselves of this opportunity to renew to the Diplomatic Missions the assurance of their highest consideration.

BRITISH EMBASSY,

···········
·····················

例 二 十 七

The Embassy of the Republic of China presents its compliments to the Apostolic Nunciature and has the honor to acknowledge the latter's memorandum of ··········, informing the Embassy that the Right Reverend Monsignor ··············, Auditor of the First Class of the Apostolic Nunciature, has been promoted by the Holy See to the rank of Counsellor, with the title of Domestic Prelate.

例 二 十 八

The Canadian Embassy presents its compliments to the Diplomatic Missions accredited in ·········· and has the honour to inform them that Mr. ··········, First Secretary of the Embassy, has been accorded the rank of Counsellor from March 20, 1959.

The Canadian Embassy avails itself of this opportunity to renew to the Diplomatic Missions accredited in ·········· the assurances of its highest consideration.

··············.··········

例 二 十 九

L'Ambassade d'Espagne présents ses compliment aux Missions Diplomatiques accréditées à ·········· et a l'honneur de porter à leur connaissance que le Marquis de ···········, ayant été promu au rang de Ministre Plénipotentiaire, continuera à assumer les fonctions de Conseiller de cette Ambassade sous le titre de Ministre Conseiller.

L'Ambassade d'Espagne saisit cette occasion pour renouveler aux Missions Diplomatiques accréditées à ········ les assurances de sa très haute considération.

······························

例 三 十

La Légation de Chine présente ses compliments très empressés à la Direction Générale du Protocole, Ministère des Affaires Etrangères et a l'honneur de L'informer que Mr. ···········, troisième Secrétaire de cette Légation, est arrivé le ··········· à son poste.

Cette Légation sera trés obligée à la Direction Générale du Protocole de vouloir bien l'insérer dans la prochaine édition de la Liste du Corps Diplomatique.

······························

················

例 三 十 一

L'Ambassade de ·········· présente ses compliments aux
Missions Diplomatiques accréditées en ··········· et a l'honneur
de porter à leur connaissance que Monsieur ···········, ci–devant
Conseiller de Presse près cette Ambassade, ayant été appelé à
d'autres fonctions a quitté ··········· et que Monsieur ···········,
nommé Conseiller de Presse prsès cette Ambassade, est arrivé
à ··········· et a pris possession de ses fonctions.

··

AUX MISSIONS DIPLOMATIQUES
 ACCREDITEES EN ···········

例 三 十 二

L'Ambassade de France Présente ses compliments à
l'Ambassade de Chine et a l'honneur de lui faire savoir que
M. ···········, a été nommé Secrétaire d'Ambassade, chargé des
affaires culturelles et commerciales à l'Ambassade de France.
 M. ··········· a pris son service le premier mars. Il sera
inscrit sur la liste du personnel à la suite de M.···········%

··

五、離　　任

Departure from Post

　　如使節因任期屆滿，或任務終了，或奉命囘國服務，或奉調轉赴他國任所，或辭職奉准，或年老退休，或其他原因，臨行時除依照習慣參加惜別，及向駐在國政府元首呈遞辭任國書外，並應備文通知駐在國外交部部長及其他國家使節，謂在新任使節未到任前，館務指定首席館員某某暫行代理。最後並表示對在任時公務與私交關係均愉快，將永誌不忘等字樣。

　　在此處有一點須特別提到的，卽駐在同一首都的新舊兩使節，事實上因不能在任所直接辦理交接，所以舊任離任時，必須指派館員暫代館務。全權大使或公使依法全權代表國家元首或國家，故一個國家在一個時期僅有一個法定代表，在他未離開駐在國國土前，新使節多不到任。

　　如平時因事或休假離開任所，照例亦應通知駐在國外交部及駐在同地之他國使館，並說明已指定館員某某代理館務，此項被指定臨時代館之人員稱 CHARGE D'AFFAIRES *ad interim,* 通知文件用節略。

　　外交部部長如因事出國，外交部應備節略通知駐在該國之各國使館，在節略中須說明部務由何人代理（見本節例二十二）。

　　有使館除館長及一二僱員外，根本無館員可指定代理館務者，在此種情形下可託友邦使館館長代爲照拂其館務，如前比利時駐菲律賓公使館，除公使外卽無館員，故該公使於一九五六年因事離菲時，卽託荷蘭駐菲公使代爲照拂比國公使館館務（見本節例十八）。

　　至一般館員奉調囘國，或轉調他館，例由原服務之使館備文通知駐在國外交部及其他使館，行文格式多用節略。

　　茲將所舉各例分館長離任，館長短期離開任所及館員離任三類列之。

舘 長 離 任

Chiefs of Mission

例 一

Excellency:

I have the honor to inform Your Excellency that I will be leaving ·········· tomorrow, ··········, 1957.

After my departure and until the arrival of my successor, Mr. ·········· will be in charge of this Embassy in the capacity of Chargé d'Affaires *ad interim*.

I wish to express to you my sincere thanks for what you have done to maintain the friendly relations which exist between our two Missions, and to assure you that I shall remember with much pleasure our association at this post.

Please accept, Excellency, the assurances of my highest consideration.

(signed)··························

例 二

Your Excellency:

I have the honour to inform you that, having been appointed to another post, I shall be leaving ·········· on the··········

Pending the arrival of my successor Mr. ·········· on or about the ········, this Mission will be in charge of Mr.········, Third Secretary of this Legation.

In taking leave of you, I desire to express my cordial thanks for all that you have done to maintain the excellent relations which exist between our two Missions, and to assure you that I shall always look back with pleasure on the period which I have been privileged to work with you in ··········

I avail myself of this opportunity, Your Excellency, of renewing the assurance of my very highest consideration.

(Signed) ··························

Excellency,

I have the honour to inform Your Excellency that, having completed my mission as Minister of Belgium to the ··········, I am leaving ··········· on ···········

Until my successor arrives, Mr. ··········· will be in charge as "Chargé des Affaires Courantes de la Légation de Belgique".

I shall remember with the greatest of pleasure the friendly relations which I have had the privilege of maintaining with Your Excellency during my stay in··········, and I take this opportunity to express my very best wishes for the continued success of Your Excellency's mission in the ·········

Please accept, Excellency, the renewed assurances of my highest consideration.

(Signed) Belgian Minister

His Excellency ·······················

Ambassador Extraordinary and Plenipotentiary

of the Republic of ···········

·····················

例　　四

甲使節與乙使節所代表之政府間本無邦交，或邦交因事暫行中斷，在外交團似仍應保持相當之關係。如下例英國大使離任時仍照例行文暫無邦交之領袖大使告別，雖文中第二段僅提及 personal relations，然已表明兩使節間關係之不惡。

Your Excellency,

I have the honour to inform Your Excellency that I am leaving ………… to–day on relinquishing the post of Her Britannic Majesty's Ambassador to …………. Pending the arrival of my successor, Mr. …………, Counsellor, will be in charge of the Embassy in the capacity of Chargé d'Affaires *ad interim*.

On relinquishing my post, I should like to express to Your Excellency my appreciation of the excellent personal relations which have existed between us and which I shall remember with much pleasure.

I avail myself of this opportunity to renew to Your Excellency the assurance of my highest consideration.

(Signed) …………………………

His Excellency

　　……………………,

　　Dean of the Diplomatic Corps,

　　En Ville.

Monsieur le Ministre,

J'ai l'honneur de porter à la connaissance de Votre Excellence qu'ayant présenté ma démission, qui a été acceptée, je quitte aujourd'hui ···········

Jusqu'à l'arrivée de mon successeur la Légation Royale de Bulgarie sera gérée par Monsieur············, Conseiller de Légation, en qualité de Chargé d'Affaires a. i.

Au moment de prendre congé de Votre Excellence, il m'est particulièrement agréable de Lui exprimer tout le plaisir que j'ai eu d'entretenir avec Elle des relations empreintes de sympathie et de cordialité. Je prie Votre Excellence de vouloir bien croire que j'en garderai le meilleur souvenir.

Veuillez agréer, Monsieur le Ministre, les assurances de ma haute considération.

(signature)

六

Monsieur le Ministre,

J'ai l'honneur de porter à Votre connaissance qu'ayant été nommé Ambassadeur de Pologne aux Etats Unis d'Amérique, je quitte aujourd'hui ···········

Jusqu'à l'arrivée de mon successeur ···········, Monsieur ···········, Conseiller de L'Ambassade, gérera les affaires de l'Ambassade en qualité de Chargé d'Affaires a.i.

Au moment de prendre congé, il m'est particulièrement agréable de Vous exprimer le vif plaisir que j'ai éprouvé à entretenir avec Vous des relations amicales et sincères.

Je tiens à Vous assurer que j'en garderai toujours le meilleur souvenir.

Veuillez agréer, Monsieur le Ministre, les assurances de ma haute considération.

....

S.E.
  Monsieur·······················
    Envoyé Extraordinaire et Ministre
      Plénipotentiaire de············
        ·····················.····

例　　　　七

Monsieur l'Ambassadeur,

Au moment de quitter············, j'ai l'honneur de remercier Votre Excellence du soin attentif qu'Elle a pris d'entretenir entre nos Missions les relations les plus cordiales et d'établir entre nous les rapports personnels les plus confiants.

Je forme le souhait que ces rapports en perdant leur caractère officiel conserveront dans l'avenir la même cordialité que dans le passé.

Monsieur ··············, Conseiller de l'Ambassade, assumera jusqu'à l'arrivée de mon successeur, la direction de cette Ambassade en qualité de Chargé d'Affaires a.i.

Je vous prie d'agréer, Monsieur l'Ambassadeur, les assurances de ma très haute considération.

(signed)······················

Monsieur l'Ambassadeur,

J'ai l'honneur de porter à la connaissance de Votre Excellance que je quitterai ·········· le ···········, sur l'achèvement de la période de mon service comme Ambassadeur des Etats-Unis d'Amerique en ···········. Jusqu'à l'arrivée de mon successeur, l'Ambassade sera gérée par Monsieur·········, Conseiller d'Ambassade, en qualité de Chargé d'Affaires ad interim.

Permettez-moi d'exprimer, au moment de mon départ, la très sincère satisfaction que j'ai éprouvée dans nos relations, tant personnelles qu'officielles, lesquelles ont été invariablement amicales et cordialles- Je garderai toujours le meilleur souvenir de ces rapports.

Veuillez agréer, Monsieur l'Ambassadeur, les assurances de ma très haute considération.

....

Monsieur l'Ambassadeur,

J'ai l'honneur de porter à la connaissance de Votre Excellence qu'ayant été appelé à mon Ministère à la Haye, je quitte aujourd'hui définitivement ·········· en laissant, jusqu'à la prise de service de mon successeur, la gérance de l'Ambassade à Monsieur ········, Secrétaire d'Ambassade, en qualité de Chargé d'affaires a.i.

En prenant congé de Votre Excellence à la fin de mon séjour en Grèce, je tiens à Vous remercier du soin attentif que Vous avez pris d'entretenir entre nos deux missions les

meilleurs relations et d'établir entre nous les rapports personnels les plus confiants.

Je me flatte de l'espoir que ces rapports, en perdant leur
caractère officiel, n'en conserveront pas moins dans l'avenir la
même cordialité que dans le passé.

Veuillez agréer, Monsieur l'Ambassadeur, les assurances
de ma très haute considération.

(Signed) ·····················

····················

例　　十

Au Ministre des Affaires Etrangères

et

à toutes les Missions Diplomatiques

J'ai l'honneur de porter à la connaissance de Votre Excellence qu'ayant été appelé à assumer les fonctions de Juge à la
Cour Internationale de Justice, je quitte définitivement···········

Monsieur········, Conseiller, gérera les affaires de l'Ambassade jusqu'à l'arrivée de mon successeur, en qualité de Chargé
d'Affaires a.i.

Au moment où ma mission dans ce pays prend fin, je suis
heureux d'exprimer à Votre Excellence le très vif plaisir que
j'ai eu à entretenir avec Elle d'aussi excellentes relations tant
officielles que personnelles dont je conserverai le meilleur
souvenir.

Veuillez ···········.

Monsieur l'Ambassadeur,

J'ai l'honneur de porter à la connaissance de Votre Excellence qu'ayant été appelé à exercer des nouvelles fonctions je quitte définitivement ·············· aujourd'hui et que, jusqu'à l'arrivée de mon successeur, Monsieur ············, Secrétaire, assumera la direction de cette Mission Diplomatique en qualité de Chargé d'Affaires a.i.

Au moment où ma mission en ············ prend fin, je tiens à exprimer à Votre Excellence la très sincère satisfaction que j'ai éprouvée à maintenir avec Elle les plus cordiales relations, tant personnelles qu'officielles, dont je garderai toujours le meilleur souvenir.

Veuillez agréer, Monsieur l'Ambassadeur, les assurances de ma plus haute considération.

(Signed) ·····················

Son Excellence ············
　Ambassadeur Extraordinaire et
　　Plénipotentiaire de ············
　　　En Ville.

Monsieur le Ministre,

Nommé par mon Gouvernement à l'Ambassade de France à ············, je dois rejoindre dans un très bref délai le poste qui vient de m'être confié et regrette vivement de ne pouvoir, avant mon départ, prendre congé de vous.

Il m'aurait été particulièrement agréable de vous dire quel

souvenir j'emporte des relation amicales que nous avons eues pendant ma mission en ············ et que mon successeur ne manquera pas, j'en suis assuré, de poursuivre et d'entretenir à son tour.

Veuillez agréer, Monsieur le Ministre, les assurances de ma haute considération.

(signed) ·······················

例　十　三

館長通知離任，館務暫交由館員代理，受文使館之館長復文即可直接文復代館之臨時代辦，其形式如下：

Monsieur le Chargé d'Affaires,

J'ai l'honneur d'accuser réception de la lettre de Son Excellence Monsieur le Ministré de Bulgarie en date du 3 courant par laquelle Elle a bien voulu me faire connaître qu'Elle devait quitter définitivement la ············ ce jour même et que jusqu'à l'arrivée de Son successeur vous assuriez la gérance de la Légation Royale en qualité de Chargé d'Affaires.

Veuillez agréér, Monsieur le Chargé d'Affaires, les assurances de ma haute considération.

·······························

Monsieur ············,
　　Chargé d'Affaires a.i.
　　　de la Légation Royale de Bulgarie.
　　　En Ville.

例 十 四

代辦離任，該代辦之政府另任命新使節接任，在此種情形下該代辦於離任時可備文通知駐在地各館館長，其形式如下：

Monsieur l'Ambassadeur,

J'ai l'honneur d'informer Votre Excellence que j'ai transmis aujourd'hui la gérance de cette Légation à Monsieur le Dr. …………, qui a été nommé Ministre de Portugal à …………

Au moment de finir l'accomplissement des fonctions que le Gouvernement de mon pays a fait l'honneur de me confier, comme Chargé d'Affaires de Portugal à …………, c'est pour moi un agréable devoir de Vous assurer que les délicates attentions, que Votre Excellence a bien voulu m'accorder officiellement et dans nos relations personnelles, me rappelleront toujours de Vos hautes qualités.

Je saisis cette occasion pour renouveler à Votre Excellence, Monsieur l'Ambassadeur, l'assurance de ma plus haute considération.

(signed)…………………

舘長短期離任

Temporaty Absence of Chiefs of Mission

例 十 五

The Australian Ambassador presents his compliments to His Excellency the Ambassador of the Republic of .... and has the honour to state that he will be absent from .... from ...., to ...., on an official visit to............. During his absence, Mr. ...., First Secretary, will act as Chargé d'Affaires ad interim.

The Australian Ambassador avails himself of this opportunity to renew to His Excellency the Ambassador of the Republic of............the assurance of his highest consideration.

例 十 六

Mr. Ambassador,

I have the honor to inform you that I am leaving today for a brief visit abroad and that until my return Mr............., Counselor of Embassy, will assume charge of the Embassy in the capacity of Charge d'Affaires ad interim.

Please accept, Mr. Ambassador, the assurances of my highest consideration.

....

例 十 七

December 3, 1956.

Your Excellency,

I have the honour to inform Your Excellency that Her Britannic Majesty's Ambassador left ·········· on December 2 for a short visit to London and that, during the absence of Sir ··········, I shall be in charge of Her Majesty's Embassy.

I avail myself of this opportunity to renew to Your Excellency, the assurance of my highest esteem.

(Sgn.)···························

His Excellency Monsieur···········,

  Embassy of the Republic of···········,

   En Ville.

例 十 八

The Belgian Legation presents its compliments to the Chinese Embassy and has the honor to inform the latter that Mr.···········, Minister of Belgium, has left today for ···········, and that as of this date and during his absence, His Excellency ···········, Minister of the Netherlands, will take charge of this Legation.

······················

復　　文

The Embassy of the Republic of China presents its compliments to the Legation of Belgium and has the honor to acknowledge the receipt of the latter's memorandum of·········, informing the Embassy that His Excellency ··········· has left for ········· and that during his absence, His Excellency ·········, Minister of the Netherlands, will take charge of the Legation. ·····················

例　十　九

Monsieur l'Ambassadeur,

J'ai l'honneur de faire savoir à Votre Excellence que je quitte aujourd'hui ···········, me rendant en congé en France.

Monsieur·········, Conseiller de l'Ambassade, me remplacera en qualité de Chargé d'Affaires a.i.

Je vous prie d'agréer, Monsieur l'Ambassadeur, les assurances de ma très haute considération.

(French Ambassador)

例　二　十

Monsieur l'Ambassadeur,

J'ai l'honneur de porter à la connaissance de Votre Excellence que je pars aujourd'hui pour un bref séjour à l'étranger et que pendant mon. absence Monsieur ··············, gérera la Légation en qualité de Chargé d'Affaires a.i.

Veuillez agréer, Monsieur l'Ambassadeur, les assurances de ma très haute considération.

(signature)

例 二 十 一

通知代館之復文

Monsieur le Chargé d'Affaires,

J'ai l'honneur d'accuser réception de la lettre No. ⋯⋯⋯⋯
que Son Excellence le Ministre de Danemark, Monsieur⋯⋯⋯
a bien voulu m'adresser en date du ⋯⋯⋯⋯ pour m'informer
qu'il quittait le même jour ⋯⋯⋯⋯ pour se rendre en voyage
à l'étranger et que pendant son absence, la Légation Royale
serait gérée par vous en qualité de Chargé d'Affaires a.i.

Je prends acte de cette aimable communication et je
saisis cette occasion pour vous renouveler, Monsieur le
Chargé d'Affaires, les assurances de ma considération la plus
distinguée,

例 二 十 二

外交部長因公出國，外交部須用節略通知各外國使館，部務暫由
次長代理。

The Chief of Protocol presents his compliments to Their
Excellencies and Messieurs the Chiefs of Mission and has the
honor to inform that the Honorable ⋯⋯⋯⋯, Vice President
and concurrently Secretary of Foreign Affairs, departed today
for ⋯⋯⋯⋯, to attend the annual meeting of the Council of
Ministers of the Southeast Asia Collective Defense Treaty
Organization, and that he is expected to return on or about
⋯⋯⋯⋯.

During the absence of the Secretary, the Honorable⋯⋯⋯
will be the Acting Secretary of Foreign Affairs.

復　文

The Ambassador of the Republic of ·········· presents his compliments to the chief of Protocol and has the honor to acknowledge the receipt of the latter's memorandum of·········, informing that the Honorable ··············, Vice president and concurrently Secretary of Foreign Affairs, departed on ········· for············, to attend the annual meeting of the Council of Ministers of the Southeast Asia Collective Defense Treaty Organization and that during the absence of the Secretary, the Honorable ············ will be the Acting Secretary of Foreign Affairs.

例　二　十　三

外交部長公畢囘國，應即銷假視事。

The Chief of Protocol of the Department of Foreign Affairs presents his compliments to Their Excellencies and Messieurs the Chiefs of Mission and has the honor to inform that the Honorable ········, Secretary of Foreign Affairs of the Republic of ············, returned to Manila on Sunday morning, ············, and has resumed his duties as Secretary of Foreign Affairs.

The Honorable ···············, who was designated Acting Secretary of Foreign Affairs during the absence of Secretary ············, has reverted to his former position as Undersecretary of Foreign Affairs.

例 二 十 四

館長囘館銷假，繼續主持館務，應再通知各國使館，其格式如下：

Monsieur l'Ambassadeur,

J'ai l'honneur de faire savoir à Votre Excellence que rentré aujourd'hui à ·········· j'ai repris la direction de cette Ambassade.

Je vous prie d'agréer, Monsieur l'Ambassadeur, les assuronces de ma très haute considération.

(signed) French Ambassador

例 二 十 五

Note–Circulaire
······················

L'Ambassade Impériale d'Ethiopie présente ses compliments aux Missions Diplomatiques accréditées à ·········· et a l'honneur de porter à leur connaissance que Son Excellence ·········, Ambassadeur d'Ethiopie, est rentré aujourd'hui à ·········· et a repris la direction de cette Ambassade Impériale.

L'Ambassade Impériale d'Ethiopie saisit l'occasion pour réitérer aux Missions Diplomatiques accréditées à ·········· les assurances de sa très haute considération.

···································

Aux
Missions Diplomatiques
accréditées à
······················

例 二 十 六

通知回館之復文

....

Monsieur le Ministre,

J'ai l'honneur, Excellence, d'accuser réception de Votre
lettre No ·········· de ··········, par laquelle Vous avez bien
voulu m'informer que, de retour en ··········, Vous avez repris
la direction de la Légation.

Je Vous remercie, Monsieur le Ministre, de cette obligeante
communication dont je prends acte, et je saisis cette occasion
pour vous renouveler les assurances de ma haute considération.

(signature)

Son Excellence
   Monsieur le Dr. ··········
      Envoyé Extraordinaire et Ministre
         Plénipotentiaire des
            ···················

館 員 離 任

Staff Members of Mission

例 二 十 七

The Canadian Embassy presents its compliments to Diplomatic Missions in ·········· and has the honour to inform them
of the departure on June 4 of Mr. ··········, Second Secretary,
who is proceeding to a new post at the Canadian Legation,
Lisbon, Portugal.

例 二 十 八

L'Ambassade de Chine présente ses compliments au Ministére Royal des Affaires Etrangères et a l'honneur de porter à
Sa connaissance que Monsieur ············, conseiller de cette
Ambassade, est appelé à assumer d'autres fonctions et quittera
définitivement ············ le ············.

L'Ambassade de Chine saisit cette occasion pour renouveler
au Ministère Royal des Affaires Etrangères les assurances de
sa très haute considération.

······································

例 二 十 九
Note Circulaire

······························

L'Ambassade de la République Fédérale d'Allemagne
présente ses compliments à l'Ambassade de············et a l'honneur de Lui faire savoir que Monsieur ············, Conseiller de
cette Ambassade, fut transféré à une autre destination.

Elle saisit cette occasion pour renouveler à l'Ambassade
de ············ les assurances de sa très haute considération.

······································

例 三 十

L'Ambassade de France présente ses compliments aux
Missions Diplomatiques accréditées à ············ et a l'honneur
de leur faire savoir que Monsieur ············, Conseiller Commercial
prés cette Ambassade, a quitté définitivement ············ le 15
mai et a été remplacé par Monsieur············.

Monsieur ············ est accompagné de son épouse.

L'Ambassade de France saisit cette occasion pour renouveler aux Missions Diplomatiques accréditées à ············, les
assurances de sa très haute considération.

······································

六、國　　書
Credentials

國書普通分到任國書 CREDENTIALS 或 LETTER OF CREDENCE 與辭任國書 LETTER OF RECALL 兩種，到任國書乃一國元首派駐使節至對方國所用之國家正式文書，爲一種信任狀，由派使國元首署名，並由其外交部長副署，爲使節到任時呈遞駐在國元首之用。辭任國書則爲使節任滿告辭時向駐在國元首呈遞之用。依照我國慣例，國書正副本均用中文書寫另斟酌情形備英文或法文或西班牙文等外文譯本。正本封口，備於呈遞時親自面呈，副本開口，備事先送交外交部長，供其參考。

在君主國家如元首死亡或國王更換，照例須重發國書，重新呈遞，外國政府派駐該國之使節亦然。如爲民主國家，則總統之更換，並不影響國書之效力，其理由是主權在民，故民主國家更換元首，毋須重發國書，亦毋須再行呈遞新國書，這種習慣中美等國皆遵行有年。

如一國元首派一外交代表或代表團負責商訂條約，或參加國際會議，其目的在達成協議。代表之權限若何，普通皆須由其本國政府明白授予，此項授權證書通稱爲全權證書 FULL POWERS. 在簽訂條約之前通常皆須交驗全權證書。如爲一國際會議，參與會議各代表之全權證書均須交由一特別組成之委員會審查通過。

除上述國書外，在本節另附兩項文書，一爲領事委任文憑（見本節例十八例十九），一爲領事證書，前者爲本國政府發給之證書，英文稱 CONSULAR COMMISSION 或 LETTER OF PROVISION，說明派某某爲駐某地方領事，所有關係該地方本國人民種種以及商務利益，均歸該領事依法保護。領事奉到本國政府發給之委任文憑後，應經由其本國大使館或公使館送請駐在國外交部轉請頒發領事證書或領事許可證 EXEQUATUR（見本節例二十），以便行使領事官應享有之職權。

以下舉例從第一至第五爲到任國書格式，例七至例十二爲辭任國書格式，例十三例十四爲呈遞國書時頌詞及答詞格式，例十五至例十七爲全權證書格式。

到 任 國 書
Letters of Credence

例 一

LIN SEN
President of the National Government of the
Republic of China
to
HIS MAJESTY GEORGE VI
King of Great Britain, Ireland and the British Dominion
beyond the Seas, Emperor of India, etc., etc., etc.
Sendeth Greeting!

Great and good Friend:

I have made choice of Mr. Hsu Mo, former Political Vice-Minister of Foreign Affairs of the Republic of China, to reside near Your Majesty's Government in the Commonwealth of Australia in the character of Envoy Extraordinary and Minister Plenipotentiary of the Republic of China.

Mr. Hsu Mo is well informed of the relative interests of China and Australia and of the sincere desire of this Government to cultivate to the fullest extent the friendship which has so long subsisted between the two countries. My knowledge of his high character and ability gives me entire confidence that he will constantly endeavor to advance the interests and welfare of both countries and so render himself acceptable to Your Majesty. I therefore request Your Majesty's Government in the Commonwealth of Australia to receive him favorably and to give full credence to what he shall say on the part of the Republic of China.

I avail myself of this opportunity to wish good health to Your Majesty and prosperity to the Commonwealth of Australia.

Given in Chungking, the⋯⋯⋯⋯day of the⋯⋯⋯⋯month of the year of the Republic of China (⋯⋯⋯⋯, 19⋯⋯⋯⋯⋯)。

例　　二

CHIANG KAI SHEK
PRESIDENT OF THE NATIONAL GOVERNMENT
OF THE REPUBLIC OF CHINA
TO
HIS EXCELLENCY············
PRESIDENT OF THE REPUBLIC OF ············

Great and good Friend:

Being desirous of strengthening the friendly relations between the Republic of China and the Republic of············, I have made choice of Dr.············to reside near the Government of Your Excellency in the capacity of Ambassador Extra-ordinary and Plenipotentiary of China.

Having already had ample experience of Dr. ············ 's eminent qualities, I am convinced that he will fulfill the important duties of his mission in such a manner as to merit Your Excellency's approbation and esteem and to prove himself worthy of this fresh mark of my confidence.

I therefore request that Your Excellency receive Dr. ··············favorably and give full credence to all that he shall have occasion to communicate to You in the name of the National Government, more especially when he shall express to You the assurances of my sincere friendship and high esteem.

I avail myself of this opportunity to wish good health to Your Excellency and prosperity to the············nation.

Signed:　　CHIANG KAI SHEK

Countersigned: WANG SHIH CHIEH

Given at Nanking, this twelfth day of the third month of the············year of the Republic of China (March 12,············)

Our Good Friend:

Being desirous to maintain, without interruption, the relations of friendship and good understanding which happily subsist between Our Realm and the Republic of ...., We have made choice of Our Trusty and Well–beloved .... to reside with You in the character of Our Ambassador Extraordinary and Plenipotentiary.

The experience which We have had of ....'s talents and zeal for Our service assures Us that the selection We have made will be perfectly agreeable to You; and that he will discharge the important duties of his Mission in such a manner as to merit Your approbation and esteem, and to prove himself worthy of this new mark of Our confidence.

We therefore request that You will give entire credence to all that .... shall communicate to You in Our name, more especially when he shall renew to You the assurances of the lively interest which We take in everything that affects the welfare and prosperity of the Republic of.............

And so We commend You to the protection of the Almighty.

Given at Our Court of St. James, the.........day of ...., One thousand Nine hundred and ...., in the .... Year of Our Reign.

Your Good Friend,
(Signed) ELIZABETH R.

....

President of the United States of America.

To His Majesty,

Wilhelm II,

German Emperor, King of Prussia,

etc.　　　etc.　　　　etc.

Great and Good Friend:

I have made choice of Mr.············, one of our distinguished citizens, to reside near the Government of Your Majesty in the quality of Ambassador Extraordinary and Plenipotentiary of the United States of America. He is well informed of the relative interests of the two countries and of our sincere desire to cultivate to the fullest extent the friendship which has so long subsisted between us. My knowledge of his high character and ability gives me entire confidence that he will constantly endeavour to advance the interest and prosperity of both Governments, and so render himself acceptable to Your Majesty.

I, therefore, request Your Majesty to receive him favorably and to give full credence to what he shall say on the part of the United States and to the assurances which I have charged him to convey to you of the best wishes of this Government for the prosperity of the German Empire.

May God have Your Majesty in His wise Keeping.

Your Good Friend,

....

Washington. (Date.)

JOHN F. KENNEDY
President of the United States of America

To His

．．．．．．．．．．．．．．．．．．．．．．．，

President of the Republic of China.

Great and Good Friend:

I have made choice of ．．．．．．．．．．．, a distinguished citizen of the United States, to reside near the Government of Your Excellency in the quality of Ambassador Extraordinary and Plenipotentiary of the United States of America. He is well informed of the relative interests of the two countries and of the sincere desire of this Government to cultivate to the fullest extent the friendship which has so long subsisted between them. My knowledge of his high character and ability gives me entire confidence that he will constantly endeavor to advance the interests and prosperity of both Governments and so erender himself acceptable to Your Excellency.

I therefore request Your Excellency to receive him favorably and to give full credence to what he shall say on the part of the United States and to the assurances which I have charged him to convey to you of the best wishes of this Government for the prosperity of China.

May God have Your Excellency in His wise Keeping.

Your Good Friend,

By the President: /s/．．．．．．．．．．．．．．．．．．．．．．

/s/．．．．．．．．．．．．．．．．．．．

Acting Secretary of State

Washington,．．．．．．．．．．．．．．．．, 1963.

譯　本

美利堅合眾國總統……………謹致書於

中華民國總統蔣中正閣下：茲特遴派本國聲譽卓著之…………爲美利堅合眾國特命全權大使，駐劄　貴國，該使對於

貴我兩國之相互利益與本國政府亟欲增進

貴我兩國間傳統睦誼之意願，深所稔悉，且其品德優良，才猷卓越，膺斯重任，必能克盡厥職，以促進　貴我兩國政府之利益與繁榮，而得以仰邀

閣下之嘉許。故凡該使代表本國政府有所陳述，以及向

閣下申致本人代表本國政府祝頌

貴國國運昌隆之忱時，統祈

推誠相與，信任有加，是所至禱。順頌

閣下政躬康泰，永邀　天眷

　　　　　　　　　　　　　　…………………………（簽署）

　　　　　　　　　　　　　　代理國務卿（副署）

例　　六

…………共和國總統…………閣下：茲爲維持並增進

貴我兩國固有之睦誼起見，特遴派…………先生爲…………共和國特命全權公使駐劄

貴國。

…………公使才猷卓越，任事忠誠，膺斯新命，必能恪遵使命，克盡厥職。尚祈

閣下惠予接納，舉凡該使代表…………共和國政府，尤其代表本人有所陳述時，統祈推誠相與，信任有加，是所是禱。順頌

閣下政躬康泰，

貴國國運昌隆。

　　　　　　　…………共和國總統…………（簽署）

　　　　　　　…………外交部部長…………（簽署）

例　　七

Lettres de Créanc
....

CHIANG KAI SHEK
PRESIDENT DU GOUVERNEMENT NATIONAL DE LA
REPUBLIQUE DE CHINE
A
SON EXCELLENCE MONSIEUR············
PRESIDENT DE LA REPUBLIQUE············

Cher et Grand Ami:

Animé du désir de maintenir et de resserrer les bonnes relations qui existent si heureusement entre la Chine et la ··············, j'ai résolu d'élever au rang d'Ambassade la représentation diplomatique de Chine en········et d'accréditer Monsieur le Docteur ············ auprès de Votre Excellence en qualité d'Ambassadeur Extraordinaire et Plénipotentiaire.

Les qualités et les talents qui distinguent Monsieur le Docteur ···········, ainsi que son expérience et son dévouement me sont de sûrs garants qu'il s'acquittera avec zèle de la haute mission qui lui a été confiée, de manière à mériter la confiance de Votre Excellence, et par la même, mon approbation.

C'est dans cette conviction que je prie Votre Excellence de vouloir bien lui réserver un bienveillant accueil et d'ajouter foi et créance entière à toutes les communications qu'il sera appelé à Lui addresser, soit en mon nom, soit au nom du Gouvernement National de la République de Chine.

Je saisis cette occasion pour présenter à Votre Excellence mes voeux les plus sincères pour Sa santé aussi bier que pour la prospérité de···········

Fait à ···········, le Vingt–huitième jour du Onzième mois de la ··········· année de la République de Chine (28 Novembre ···········)

Signé: CHIANG KAI SHEK
Contresigné: T.V. SOONG

例　八

CHIANG KAI SHEK
PRESIDENT DU GOUVERNEMENT NATIONAL DE LA
REPUBLIQUE DE CHINE
A
SA MAJESTE IMPERIALE MOHAMMED REZA SHAH
PAHLAVI CHAHINCHAH DE L'IRAN

Cher et Grand Ami,

Animé du désir de maintenir et de resserrer les liens d'amitié qui existent si heureusement entre la Chine et l'Iran, j'ai résolu d'accréditer auprès de Votre Majesté Monsieur ······ ······en qualité d'Ambassadeur Extraordinaire et Plénipotentiaire de la République de Chine.

Les qualités qui distinguent Monsieur···········, son expérience et son dévouement me sont garants du soin qu'Il mettra à s'acquitter de la haute mission qui lui est confiée de façon à meriter Sa confiance et obtenir ainsi mon approbation.

C'est dans cette conviction que je La prie de l'accueillir avec bienveillance et d'ajouter foi et créance à tout ce qu'il aura l'honneur de Lui communiquer soit en mon nom, soit au nom du Gouvernement National de la République de Chine.

Je saisis cette occasion pour Lui exprimer les voeux les plus sincères que je forme pour Son bonheur personnel et pour la prospérité de Son pays.

Signé:　　CHIANG KAI SHEK

Contresigné: WANG SHEH CHIEH

Fait à Nankin. le vingt-sixième jour du sixième mois de la trente-cinquième année de la République de Chine.

(le 26 juin, 1946)

例 九

LETTRE DE CRÉANCE

....

Trés cher et Grand Ami,

Désireux de resserer encore d'avantage les relations de bonne intelligence qui existent si heureusement entre le Royaume de Danemark et la République Chinoise, J'ai résolu de charger Monsieur ...., de Me représenter auprès de Vous, en qualité de Mon Envoyé Extraordinaire et Ministre Plénipotentiaire. La connaissance que J'ai acquise des qualités qui distinguent Monsieur ....et de son zèle et dévouement à Mon service, Me persuade qu'il ne négligera rien pour obtenir Votre estime et Votre confiance, et dans cette conviction. Je Vous pris de l'accueuillir avec bienveillance, et d'ajouter foi et créance entière à tout ce qu'il Vous dira de Ma part, surtout lorsqu'il Vous exprimera les assurances d'estime et d'amitié avec lesquelles, Je suis

Très cher et grand Ami

Votre sincère Ami

Au

Président du Gouvernement

National de la République Chinoise

例 十

常駐代辦到任，由本國外交部部長正式備文通知駐在國政府外交部長（參閱四、到任）

Nankin, le 16 Juillet 1947.

Excellence,

J'ai l'honneur de faire savoir à Votre Excellence que le Gouvernement National de la République de Chine, animé du désir de resserrer les relations cordiales existant heureusement entre le Gouvernement Chinois et celui de la Pologne, a résolu d'accréditer Monsieur ·········· en qualité de Chargé d'Affaires auprès du Gouvernement de la République Polonaise.

Je me plais à espérer que Votre Ministère voudra bien reconnaître Monsieur ·········· dans la qualité susdite et lui accorder le puissant appui et les facilités nécessaires à l'accomplissement de ses fonctions afin que le but que mon Gouvernement se propose à accomplir par cette nomination nouvelle puisse être atteint.

Je profite de cette occasion pour exprimer à Votre Excellence les assurances de ma haute considération.

(Signé) Ministre des Affaires Etrangères

Son Excellence
Monsieur ···············
Ministre des Affaires Etrangères
de la République Polonaise
Varsovie

例 十 一

政府派外交部次長以特使名義代表政府
參加友邦獨立慶典及正副總統就職典禮

My dear Mr. President,

I have the honour to inform Your Excellency that I have made choice of Dr.············, Political Vice-Minister of Foreign Affairs of the Republic of China, to assist as Ambassador Extraordinary on Special Mission at the ceremonies marking the proclamation of the independence of the Republic of········ and the inauguration of Your Excellency and Mr. ············as President and Vice-President. I take great pleasure in charging to You and Your Government and people my hearty congratulations as well as those of the Chinese Government and people.

The Chinese and ············ peoples have long been bound together by common ideals of peace and justice and have been good neighbours for many decades. Our traditional ties of friendship in the past should form a firm basis for mutual understanding and cooperation between the two countries in the future.

On this auspicious occasion of the founding of the············ Republic, I recall vividly the heroic struggle carried on by the ············people against the Japanese invaders in the last world war. As a result of their indomitable will and their strenuous efforts in fighting for their freedom, they have, with the assistance of their great ally the United States of America, at last achieved the independence of their country which they fully deserved. In this connection, I am happy to think that the overseas Chinese residing in your country have contributed and will be able to continue to contribute their proper share to the building of the new············nation. I am sure that with the able leadership of Your Excellency and the united efforts of your people, the Republic of ············ will make gigantic strides of progress and assume an important place in the family of nations.

The Chinese Government is pleased with the forthcoming establishment of normal diplomatic relations between our two countries and it is my sincere hope that our peoples will henceforth cooperate closely with each other and with the other United Nations in the enhancement of our mutual interests and the accomplishment of our joint task of building a lasting peace.

I avail myself of this opportunity to extend to Your Excellency my best wishes for the prosperity of the Republic of············and the success of Your administration.

（Signed）···························

（Countersigned）···························

例　十　二

派駐在國大使爲慶賀新總統就職特使之電文

Ambassador ·················
Sinoembasy
Buenos Aires
Transmit to His Excellency ·······································,
President of the Argentine Republic, following Letter of Credence from President Chiang Kai-shek Quote

I have the honour to inform Your Excellency that I have made choice of Dr.············, Chinese Ambassador to Argentine, to assist as Ambassador Extraordinary on Special Mission at the inauguration of the new President of the Argentine Republic, His Excellency General ············, in order to convey to him my sincere friendship and high esteem.

I avail myself of this opportunity to express to Your Excellency my best wishes for your good health and the prosperity of the Argentine nation. Chiang Kai-shek President of the National Government of the Republic of China. Unquote Waichiaopu.

辭 任 國 書
Letters of Recall

辭任國書在今日國際慣例中多不親自遞交，而由繼任之使節於呈遞其到任國書時代爲呈遞，其形式如次。

例 十 三

CHIANG KAI SHEK
PRESIDENT OF THE NATIONAL GOVERNMENT
OF THE REPUBLIC OF CHINA
TO
HIS EXCELLENCY···········
PRESIDENT OF THE REPUBLIC OF···········

Great and Good Friend:

Having need elsewhere for the services of Dr. ···········,
who has for some time past resided near the Government of
Your Excellency in the quality of Ambassador Extraordinary
and Plenipotentiary of China, I have thought fit to notify to
You his recall. Dr. ··········· having resigned his mission and
being unable to present his letters of recall in person, I have
entrusted to his successor the duty of placing them in the
hands of Your Excellency.

I am satisfied with the zeal and ability with which Dr.
··········· during his mission devoted all his efforts to strengthen the good understanding and the friendly relations between
China and···········, and I entertain the hope that his conduct
will also have merited Your approbation. It is in this pleasing
confidence that I avail myself of the present opportunity to
renew to You the assurances of my best wishes for the personal
welfare of Your Excellency and the prosperity of the···········
nation.

Signed: CHIANG KAI SHEK
Countersigned: WANG SHIH CHIEH
Given at Nanking the twelfth day of the third month of
the···········year of the Republic of China (March 12,······)

例 十 四

To His Excellency

Generalissimo Chiang Kai-Shek

President of the National Government

of the Republic of China.

Great and good Friend:

Major General⋯⋯⋯⋯, who has for some time past resided near the Government of Your Excellency in the character of Ambassador Extraordinary and Plenipotentiary of the United States of America, having resigned his mission and being unable to present his Letters of Recall in person, I have entrusted to his successor the duty of placing them in the hands of Your Excellency.

I am pleased to believe that General ⋯⋯⋯⋯, during his mission, devoted all his efforts to strenthening the good understanding and the friendly relations existing between the Governments of the United States and China, and I entertain the hope that while fulfilling satisfactorily the trust imposed upon him he succeeded in gaining Your Excellency's esteem and good will.

Your Good Friend.

(Signed):   HARRY S. TRUMAN

(Countersigned): Dean Acheson

例 十 五

Sir My Brother:

Having occasion elsewhere for the services of My Trusty and Well-beloved ⋯⋯⋯, who has lately resided at Your Majesty's Court in the character of My Ambassador Extraordinary and Plenipotentiary I cannot omit to inform You of his recall.

My Trusty and Well-beloved⋯⋯⋯, who has lately resided at Your Majesty's Court in the character of My Ambassador Extraordinary and Plenipotentiary, being now on the point of retiring from My Foreign Service, I cannot omit to inform You of the termination of his Mission in that capacity.

Having Myself had ample reason to be satisfied with the zeal, ability, and fidelity with which⋯⋯⋯ has executed My orders on all occasions during his Mission, I trust that Your Majesty will also have found his conduct deserving of Your approbation and esteem, and in this pleasing confidence I avail myself of the present opportunity to renew to You the assurances of the invariable friendship and cordial esteem with which I am,

Sir My Brother,
Your Majesty's
Good Sister
Elizabeth R.

Our Court of St. James,
1960.
To My Good Brother The King of⋯⋯⋯⋯

例 十 六
LETTERS OF RECALL

Victoria, by the Grace of God, of the United Kingdom of Great Britain and Ireland Queen, Defender of the Faith, Empress of India, etc., etc., etc.

To the President of the United States of America, Sendeth Greeting! Our Good Friend!

Having need elsewhere for the services of Our Right Trusty and Well–beloved Councillor Sir············, Knight Commander of Our Most Honourable Order of the Bath, who has for some time resided with You in the character of Our Envoy Extraordinary and Minister Plenipotentiary, We have thought proper to notify to You his recall. We are Ourselves so entirely satisfied with the zeal, ability and discretion with which Sir Edward Thornton has uniformly executed Our orders during his mission, by studying to promote the friendship and good understanding which happily subsist between the two Nations, and which We trust will always continue, that We cannot doubt that You will also have found his conduct deserving of Your approbation.

We gladly embrace this opportunity to assure You of the sincere interest which We take in the welfare and prosperity of the United State. And so We recommend You to the Protection of The Almighty.

Given at Our Court at Balmoral the 25th day of May, in the Year of Our Lord 1881, and in the 44th Year of Our Reigh.

Your Good Friend, Victoria, R. et. I
(Countersigned) Granville.

To Our Good Friend,
The President of the United
States of America.

....

President of the United States of America.

To His Majesty,
  Wilhelm II,
    German Emperor, King of Prussia etc., etc., etc.

Great and Good Friend:

Mr.··········, who has for some time past resided near the Government of Your Majesty in the quality of Ambassador Extraordinary and Plenipotentiary of the United States of America, having resigned his Mission, I have directed him to take leave of Your Majesty.

Mr. ··········, whose standing instructions had been to cultivate with Your Majesty's Government relations of the closest friendship, has been directed to convey to Your Majesty the assurance of the sincere desire of this Government to strengthen the friendly feeling happily subsisting between the United States and Germany.

The zeal with which he has fulfilled his former instructions leaves no doubt that he will carry out this, his last commission in a manner agreeable to Your Majesty.

Your Good Friend,

....

By the President:
  ....

    Secretary of State.
    Washington, (Date).

例 十 八
Letter of Recall
....

President of the United States of America

To His Excellency
....

President of the Republic of China.

Great and Good Friend:

......................, who has for some time resided near the Government of Your Excellency in the quality of Ambassador Extraordinary and Plenipotentiary of the United States of America, has resigned his mission and is unable to present his letter of recall in person. I have, therefore, entrusted to his successor the duty of placing it in the hands of Your Excellency.

I am pleased to believe that .... during his mission devoted all his efforts to strengthening the good understanding and the friendly relations existing between the Governments of the United States of America and the Republic of China, and I entertain the hope that while fulfilling satisfactorily the trust imposed upon him, he succeeded in gaining Your Excellency's esteem and good will.

Your Good Friend,

....

譯　　本

............總統.........謹致書於

中華民國總統蔣中正閣下：查本國前任駐　貴國特命全權大使.........業經奉准辭職，不克親遞辭任國書，茲特命其後任代爲呈遞。

　　本人深信.........於其奉使期間，已竭盡其全力而謀增進中美兩國政府間固有之瞭解與睦誼，本人殊自引慰，諒其圓滿達成所負使命之際，必已仰邀
閣下之嘉許與寵信。

例 十 九

Lettres de Rappel

....

CHANG KAI SHEK
PRESIDENT DU GOUVERNEMENT NATIONAL
DE LA REPUBLIQUE DE CHINE
A
SON EXCELLENCE MONSIEUR ···········
PRESIDENT DE LA REPUBLIQUE···········

Cher et Grand Ami:

Ayant jugé utile d'appeler à une autre destination Monsieur ···········, jusqu ici mon Envoyé Extraordinaire et Ministre Plénipotentiaire auprés de Votre Excellence, j'ai dû mettre un terme à sa mission.

Monsieur ··········· s'étant trouvé dans l'impossibilité de remettre en personne à Votre Excellence ses Lettres de Rappel, j'ai chargé Monsieur le Docteur ···········, mon Ambassadeur, de la transmission des Présentes Lettres.

Je me plais à croire que Monsieur ···········, qui durant son séjour dans Votre pays, n'a manqué aucune occasion pour témoigner à Votre Excellence du prix que j'attache au maintien et au développement des relations entre nos deux pays, a mérité aussi bien Votre confidence que mon approbation.

Je saisis cette occasion pour exprimer à Votre Excellence mes sentiments les plus sincères et les voeux que je forme pour Son bonheur personnel et pour la prospérité de la···········

Fait à ···········, Vingt–huitième jour du Onzième mois de la···········année de la République de Chine (28 Novembrè··········.).

Signé: CHIANG KAI SHEK
Contresigné: T. V. SOONG

例 二 十
Lettres de Rappel

....

CHIANG KAI SHEK
PRESIDENT DU GOUVERNMENT NATIONAL DE LA
REPUBLIQUE DE CHINE
A
SA MAJESTE IMPERIALE MOHAMMED REZA SHAH
PAHLAVI CHAHINCHAH DE L'IRAN

Cher et Grand Ami,

Ayant jugé convenable d'appeler à une autre destination Monsieur ·············· jusqu'ici mon Ambassadeur Extraordinaire et Plenipotentiaire auprès de Votre Majesté, j'ai dû mettre un terme à sa mission et chargé Monsieur··············, son successeur, de remettre entre les mains de Votre Majesté ses Lettres de Rappel.

J'aime à croire que Monsieur ············· ait fait tout son possible, pendant la durée de son séjour en l'Iran, pour mériter la bienveillance et l'estime de Votre Majesté aussi bien que pour Lui témoigner du prix que j'attache au maintien et au développement des relations qui existent entre nos deux Pays.

Je saisis cette occasion pour Lui exprimer les voeux les plus sincères que je forme pour Son bonheur personnel et pour la prospérité de Son Pays.

Signé: ·····················

Contresigné:······················

Fait à Nankin, le vingt-sixième jour du sixième mois de la trente-cinquième année de la République de Chine. (le 26 juin, 1946).

頌詞及答詞
Speeches and Replies

頌　　詞
Speeches

　　呈遞國書時新使節例致頌詞，此項頌詞須表示本人奉本國政府任命爲駐使，深引爲快，並讚揚駐在國之歷史文化或國際地位之重要，轉達本國元首對駐在國元首致敬及親善之意，又表明其本人願努力促進並加強兩國間之友好關係。如其本人以往曾在同一駐在地擔任參事秘書等職務，似亦可追述過去居留之快慰心情。茲舉頌詞及答詞實例數則如下：

例　二　十　一

Excellency:

　　I have the honor to deliver to Your Excellency the letter of credence which accredits me as Ambassador Extraordinary and Plenipotentiary of the United States of America to the Republic of China and also the letter of recall of my distinguished predecessor in that capacity, ………….

　　Your Excellency, the friendship between the American and Chinese peoples has been, and shall continue to be, a most fundamental element of my country's foreign relations. Today, our enemies strive relentlessly to undermine this traditional friendship and to replace it with distrust and hostility. They must realize that the friendship of America for China remains undiminished and that the intention of the United States to support the Chinese people's rightful representative, the Government of the Republic of China, is unwavering. They should also be aware that the American people contemplate with the greatest esteem the unstinting reciprocation by Your Excellency's Government of the friendship that the United States has extended.

Surely, Your Excellency, the nature of the relationship between our two countries imposes a great responsibility upon those who are charged with safeguarding it, and I am, for this reason, deeply mindful of the trust that the President of the United States has reposed in me by designating me as his personal representative to Your Excellency's Government. That you have so graciously welcomed me offers me great encouragement that I may enjoy your confidence in the discharge of my mission here.

Finally, may I extend to Your Excellency and through you to the Chinese people renewed expressions of the esteem and felicitations of the President of the United States and the American Government and people.

譯　　本

總統閣下：

　　茲謹將本人奉派爲美利堅合衆國駐中華民國特命全權大使之到任國書及卓越之前任…………大使之辭任國書親遞　閣下，無任榮幸。

總統閣下：中美人民間之友誼，將繼續爲敝國以往與將來對外關係最基本因素之一。吾人之敵人今日正力圖破壞此項傳統友誼，而代之以猜忌與仇視。彼等必知美國對中國之友誼始終不渝；而美國對支持中國人民合法代表之中華民國政府之意向毫無動搖。彼等尤應明瞭，美國人民對

閣下所領導下之　貴國政府對美國之深厚友誼至爲珍視。

總統閣下　貴我兩國關係之性質，賦予負責維護此項關係者以重大之責任，本人對敝國總統任命本人爲駐華大使之高度信賴，未敢或忘。

今日寵獲　閣下對本人予以如此之優遇，其對本人之鼓勵極大，並使本人深信，在奉使期間，定可仰邀　閣下之信任，完成所負之使命。

　　最後本人謹向

閣下及　貴國人民轉達敝國總統，敝國政府與人民所同申之敬意與祝頌之忱。

總　統　答　辭

大使閣下：

閣下奉　貴國總統之命，以美利堅合眾國駐華特命全權大使身份，親遞到任國書及前任大使辭任國書，本人接受之餘，無任欣忭。

貴國前任駐華大使…………先生乃爲誠篤精明卓越難得之良友，惜其因病辭職，殊爲遺憾。適承

閣下向本人轉達　貴國總統及政府與人民之友誼至意尤深感荷。尚祈閣下轉致吾人誠摯之謝悃與至意。

　　中美兩國間之關係素極友好，多年以來，　貴我兩國結爲盟友，爲同一之理想而並肩奮鬪，今日吾人正面臨同一敵人，卽共產邪惡勢力。本人深信唯有中美兩國更進一步精誠團結，堅決奮鬪，方可消滅此一邪惡勢力，而確保亞洲及全世界之和平與安全。

大使閣下，敝國人民對　貴國友情甚篤，茲

閣下駐節是邦，本人特向

閣下保證，敝國政府將與　閣下竭誠合作，並給予一切必要之支助，俾使完成所負之使命。敬頌

…………………總統政躬康泰，

貴國國運昌隆。

Translation

Mr. Ambassador:

　　It gives me great pleasure to receive from Your Excellency the Letter of Credence with which your President has accredited you as Ambassador Extraordinary and Plenipotentiary of the

United States of America to the Republic of China, together with the Letter of Recall of your distinguished predecessor, ..., who, because of his sincerity and exceptional ability, had endeared himself to the Chinese people, but who, for reasons of health, had to relinguish his post last spring.

I wish also to thank you, Mr. Ambassador, for the friendly sentiments which you have just expressed on behalf of President···········and the Government and people of the United States. These sentiments, I can assure you, are fully reciprocated.

The relations between the Republic of China and the United States of America have always been close and cordial Ever since our two nations became allies, we have shared the same ideals and have dedicated ourselves to the victory of our common cause. Today we are facing the same enemy–International Communism. I am confident that, with even closer unity between our two countries and resolute determination to uphold our common ideals, we can not only destroy the enemies of democracy, but also ensure the peace and security of Asia and of the world.

Your Excellency, I am convinced that as representative of your great country, for which the Chinese people have great respect and affection, Your Excellency will successfully fulfill the high mission entrusted to you. I wish to assure Your Excellency that the Government of the Republic of China will sincerely cooperate with you and offer you all the necessary assistance.

I take this opportunity to convey to President ···········, through Your Excellency, my sincerest wishes for his personal well–being and for the prosperity of your great nation.

例 二 十 二

頌 詞
Speech

Monsieur le President:

I have the honour, by Command of The King, my August Sovereign, to present to Your Excellency the Letters of Credence by which his Majesty has been graciously pleased to appoint me Ambassador Extraordinary and Plenipotentiary in China. I am also commanded to present to Your Excellency the Letters recalling my predecessor, Sir·············, who wishes me to express his regrets to Your Excellency for his inability, owing to circumstances, to take his leave in person.

I am at the same time commanded to renew to Your Excellency the assurances of my Sovereign's sincere wishes for the welfare and prosperity of the Chinese Republic and to convey to Your Excellency on His Majesty's behalf an expression of His esteem and regard.

I have been watching with the utmost concern and the deepest sympathy the tribulations through which Your Excellency's great country has been passing, and I take this opportunity to express my sincere hope that the skies will soon be clear and that China will be able to play a yet more important part in world affairs to which her history and her culture entitle her.

答 詞
Reply

Monsieur l'Ambassadeur,

I am most pleased to receive from Your Excellency's hands the Letters by which your August Sovereign has accredited

Your Excellency as Ambassador Extraordinary and Plenipotentiary to the National Government of the Republic of China. It is rather unfortunate that the termination of the mission of Your Excellency's able predecessor, whose Letters of Recall you have also presented, should have been brought about under regrettable circumstances.

I want to offer my most sincere thanks, Monsieur l'Ambassadeur, for those high sentiments which you have just expressed for China and myself on behalf of your Sovereign as well as on your own. China is just going through a most trying period···struggle against unprecedented hardship and suffering, but the Chinese Government and people are convinced that she is destined to attain her object of national salvation and reconstruction and to contribute her full share to world peace and prosperity.

Your Excellency's arrival in China at this moment to take up your mission for a country which is bound to China by ties of traditional friendship and mutual understanding is, indeed, of especial significance to both nations. The National Government is always ready to extend all necessary facilities to Your Excellency during your sojourn in this country.

例 二 十 三

頌　　詞

Speech

Your Excellency,

I have the honour to present to Your Excellency the Letter whereby the President of the Republic has accredited me as representative of Italy to the Government of the Republic of China.

China and Italy, both countries of ancient civilization bound by a century-old friendship have now re-established diplomatic relations after a brief interruption due to a policy persued against the feelings as well as against the interests of the Italian people who could not at that time express its opinions freely. During the last few years Italy has followed with profound admiration the heroic struggle which the Chinese people have sustained to regain their freedom and their independence under Your Excellency's leadership.

The Italian Government reaffirms through me on this occasion its firm intention to establish friendly relations with China on entirely new bases, such as will bring about the development of the political, economical and cultural relations between the two countries in an atmosphere of sincere cordiality, reciprocal respect and mutual understanding.

Italy is glad that China has taken again in the world the prominent place to which she is entitled on account of her history and of the lofty ideals for which she has fought, and hopes that after suffering so cruelly during the war she may soon complete her peaceful reconstruction.

I assure Your Excellency that both as the official representative of democratic Italy and personally as an admirer of the ancient civilization of your country and of the invaluable qualities of your people, I will make every effort to improve and render fruitful the relations between Italy and China. In this undertaking I trust I shall find the sympathy and the authoritative support of Your Excellency and of Your Excellency's Government.

Allow me to add my personal good wishes to those expressed by my Government for the prosperity of China and for your own health.

答　　詞
Reply

Monsieur l'Ambassadeur,

It is with great pleasure that I receive from Your Excellency's hands the letter by which the President of the Italian Republic accredits you as Ambassador Extraordinary and Plenipotentiary to the Republic of China.

Being highly appreciative of the remarks you have just made, I feel the deepest sympathy for the Italian people who, after passing through a long and hard ordeal during the last world war, have succeeded in bringing about the rebirth of their nation and made gigantic strides toward the goal of freedom and democracy.

The Chinese Government fully shares the desire of the Italian Government to establish friendly relations between China and Italy on entirely new bases, for it is also our sincere hope to renew and further strengthen the traditional bonds of friendship formerly existing between our two countries. The people of China will spare no effort to cooperate with the Italian people in the development of their cordial relations and in the enhancement of their common interests.

I am glad to welcome Your Excellency, a great patriot as well as a staunch champion of democracy, in your new capacity as the first representative of the Italian Republic to the Republic of China, and I wish to assure you that in the accomplishment of your high mission you can always count upon my full support and that of the Chinese Government.
Please be good enough, Monsieur l'Ambassadeur, to convey to His Excellency the President of the Italian Republic my sincere wishes for his personal welfare and the prosperity of your country.

例 二 十 四

頌 詞

抗戰前葡國公使呈遞國書時所致頌詞

主席閣下： 本公使奉本國政府簡命,充任駐紥大中華民國全權公使,得以任命國書, 並前任公使畢安琪博士卸任國書, 敬遞於閣下之手, 曷勝榮幸。本公使所尤感愉快者, 即承本國政府之特命, 爲本國政府人民對於閣下所統治世界文化最古之 貴國政府人民表示敬愛之忱。夫與貴國同時之其他各國文化, 久已湮沒於史冊之中, 中國則以二千餘年以來先哲智慧道德之影響, 加以堅忍不拔之精神, 維持其歷史之地位, 屹然特立於今日國際之林。中國應用最新方法工具, 孳孳於國際通力合作, 於以策人民精神物質之進展, 此其毅力, 實爲其民族崇實之才能, 及上述傳統精神光耀之表現。本國國家自數世紀以來, 幸得維持與貴國國家甚深友誼及互相敬愛之關係, 對於貴國之完全所負責職,無時不以友好之精神予以注意, 並望此項關係日進無疆,共謀兩國之福利, 本公使甚願主席閣下以及貴國政府於本公使繼續之努力, 惠予合作, 以期貫徹此共同之宗旨焉。謹以本國政府及本公使個人名義,

　　敬祝　貴國國運昌盛,

貴主席政躬康泰。

答 詞

公使閣下： 本日貴公使奉 貴國大總統之命, 以葡萄牙駐華特命全權公使資格, 親齎任命國書, 及前任公使辭任國書同時遞送, 本主席接受之餘, 莫名忻悅。頃承貴公使以貴國政府與國民政府及國民實心友好之意, 尤深忻感。貴公使所稱中國努力於國際之團結及合作, 以及中葡兩國自數世紀前業已肇端之親善睦誼, 爲歐西文化輸入中國之輔助, 此則尤爲本主席所感佩, 而表同情者也。貴公使令聞久著, 誠信遠孚。此次持節蒞臨, 本主席深信中葡兩國邦交, 必能日進無疆。茲有爲貴公使告者, 貴公使奉命派使此邦。於職務上應需之便利, 國民政府於可能範圍內當竭誠予以協助, 俾得完成其任務。謹以誠摯之忱, 敬祝

貴國大總統政躬康寗, 貴國國運昌盛, 貴公使旅祉綏和。

例 二 十 五

西班牙駐法大使頌詞

Monsieur le Président,

J'ai l'honneur de remettre à Votre Excellence les lettres par lesquelles S.M. le roi Don ·········· m'accrédite en qualité d'Ambassadeur Extraordinaire et Plénipotentiaire auprès du Président de la République Française.

C'est avec empressement que je saisis cette occasion solennelle pour exprimer, au nom de mon auguste Souverain, les voeux très sincères qu'il forme pour la prospérité de la France et pour le bonheur de l'homme d'État élevé par ses concitoyens à la première magistrature du pays.

Quant à moi, porté vers la France par toutes mes sympathies, j'accepte avec joie l'honorable mission de maintenir, de développer et de rendre encore plus intimes les bons rapports dèjà existants entre deux nations soeurs par la race et l'origine, par le voisinage et la communauté des intérêts.

J'apporterai tout mon zèle dans l'accomplissement d'un devoir si conforme à mes sentiments, et j'espère pouvoir compter, pour y réussir, sur la haute bienveillance de M. le Président de la République comme sur le puissant et amical concours de son gouvernement.

法總統　答詞

Monsieur l'Ambassadeur,

Je remercie S.M. le roi d'Espagne des voeux que vous m'apportez en son nom pour la France et pour le President de la République. J'ai eu récemment l'honneur de dire à votre illustre prédécesseur, et je saisis avec empressement cette nouvelle occasion de répéter, combien je désire ardemment le bonheur de la noble nation espagnole et de son auguste Souverain.

Pour vour, monsieur l'Ambassadeur, qui connaissez la France, et qui en parlez si affectueusement, soyez persuadé qu'elle vous accueillera avec une vive sympathie et que vous trouverez auprès de son gouvernement, dans l'accomplissement de votre mission, tout le concours et toute la cordialité que vous pouvez souhaiter.

例 二 十 六

土耳其駐華大使呈遞到任國書頌詞

Excellence,

J'ai l'honneur de remettre entre les mains de Votre Excellence les lettres par lesquelles Monsieur le Président de la République Turquie, Celâl Bayar, a bien voulu m'accréditer auprès de Votre Excellence en qualité d'Ambassadeur Extraordinaire et Plénipotentiaire de Turquie.

Le Président de la République m'a en outre Chargé de présenter à Votre Excellence Ses salutations amicales et personnelles ainsi que les voeux chaleureux qu'Il forme pour le bonheur de Votre Excellence et pour la prospérité et l'avenir du peuple Chinois.

Le peuple turc éprouve à l'égard du peuple Chinois une sympathie et une amitié qui trouvent leur racine dans un long passé historique. Il a suivi avec une profonde admiration la lutte menée par le vaillant peuple Chinois pour sauvegarder son indépendence et sa dignite nationale. L'énergie et la détermination dont il fait preuve dans cette lutte héroique pour le maintien de son indépendence et pour la sauvegarde des bases d'un avenir prospère et brillant attirent du reste le respect du monde libre tout entier.

Excellence, Les liens qui unissent nos peuples sont multiples et vigoureux. Ils s'étendent à presque tous les domaines de l'activité humaine. La tâche qui m'incombera avant tout sera de veiller à ce que ces liens se renforcent encore davantage dans l'avenir. Je m'attacherai à cette tâche avec tout mon zèle et j'emploierai toute mon énergie pour approfondir les relations d'amitié qui existent déjà si heureusement entre nos deux peuples. J'ose espérer que dans l'accomplissement de cette tâche précieuse je pourrai compter sur la confiance et l'appui de Votre Excellence ainsi que du Gouvernement Chinois.

譯　　文

總統閣下：

　　本大使奉本國總統巴雅爾之命，充任土耳其共和國駐中華民國特命全權大使，謹將本人到任國書賚呈
閣下，實深榮幸。
本人總統特囑本人向　閣下代致其誠懇之敬意，並祝
閣下政躬康泰，貴國國運昌隆。
土耳其人民對　貴國人民之敬仰及友好，由來已久，對
貴國人民爲維護民族獨立國家尊嚴之努力，素極欽佩。
貴國人民爲爭取獨立而作此歷史性之英勇奮鬪，其堅毅不拔之精神，
已贏得整個自由世界之崇敬。
總統閣下，貴我兩國間之關係，密切強固，廣被各種方面。本人之任務爲加強兩國固有之友誼，自當竭力以赴，深信爲達成此項珍貴任務，必獲
閣下及貴國政府之信賴與支持。

總 統 答 詞

大使閣下：

閣下奉貴國總統之命，以土耳其共和國駐華特命全權大使身份呈遞到任國書，本總統接受之餘，無任歡忭，並承轉達

貴國總統及人民對於中華民國與本總統之盛意隆情，尤深感荷。頃閣下所稱貴我兩國關係密切，休戚相關，本總統亦深有同感。

貴我兩國之關係，因具有共同信念，益臻敦睦，而中土邦交之增進以及貴我兩國對自由世界之貢獻，實有賴於

貴國人民維護正義和平之努力及

貴國總統之英明領導。請代達本總統誠摯之友情與敬意。本總統並願乘此時機向

閣下保證本總統與本國政府將給予

閣下一切之合作，俾便　閣下完成崇高之任務，茲代表中華民國政府與人民恭祝

貴國總統政躬康泰，

貴國國運昌隆。

例 二 十 七

全 權 證 書

Full Powers　　……字第……號

中華民國總統為發給全權證書事查聯合國大會第二十屆常會曾於中華民國五十四年（公曆一九六五年）……月……日通過消除一切形式種族歧視國際公約本總統茲特派中華民國駐聯合國常任代表…………為簽署該公約之全權代表該代表以中華民國政府名義簽署之上述公約如經本總統批准定予施行為此發給證書以昭信守此證

　　　　　　簽署消除一切形式種族歧視國際公約…………收執
　　右給　全權代表中華民國駐聯合國常任代表

　　　　　　　　　中華民國總統……………

　　　　　　　　　外交部部長……………

中華民國…………年………月………日　於台北

例 二 十 八

英國女王發給之全權證書

Elizabeth the Second, by the Grace of God of the United Kingdom of Great Britain and Northern Ireland and of Her othet Realms and Territories Queen, Head of the Commonwealth, Defender of the Faith, &c., &c., &c. To all and singular to whom these Presents shall come, Greeting!

Whereas, for the better treating of and arranging any matters which are now in discussion, or which may come into discussion, between Us, in respect of Our United Kingdom of Great Britain and Northern Ireland and any other Powers or States, We have judged it expedient to invest a fit person with Full Power to conduct negotiations on Our part in respect of Our United Kingdom of Great Britain and Northern Ireland: Know ye, therefore, that We, reposing especial Trust and Confidence in the Wisdom, Loyalty, Diligence, and Circumspection of Our·········have named, made, constituted and appointed, as We do by these Presents name, make, constitute and appoint him Our undoubted Commissioner, Procurator and Plenipotentiary in respect of Our United Kingdom of Great Britain and Northern Ireland; Giving to him all manner of Power and Authority to treat, adjust and conclude with such Ministers, Commissioners or plenipotentiaries as may be vested with similar Power and Authority, on the part of any other Powers or States, any Treaty, Convention, Agreement, Protocol or other Instrument between Us and such Powers or States, and to sign for Us, and in Our name, in respect of Our United Kingdom of Great Britain and Northern Ireland, everything so agreed upon and concluded, and to do and transact all such other matters as may appertain thereto, in as ample manner and form, and with equal force and efficacy, as We Ourselves could do, if personally present: Engaging and Promising, upon Our Royal Word, that whatever things shall be so transacted and concluded by Our said Commissioner, Procurator and Plenipotentiary, in respect of Our United Kingdom of Great Britain and Northern Ireland, shall, subject it necessary to Our Ratification, be agreed to, acknowledged and accepted by Us in the fullest manner, and that We will never suffer, either in the whole or in part, any person whatsoever to infringe the same, or act contrary thereto, as far as it lies in Our power.

In witness whereof We have caused Our Great Seal to be affixed to these Presents, which We have signed with Our Royal Hand.

Given at Our Court of St. James, the⋯⋯⋯⋯day of⋯⋯⋯⋯ in the Year of Our Lord, One Thousand Nine hundred and ⋯⋯⋯⋯and in the⋯⋯⋯⋯Year of Our Reign.

例 二 十 九

FULL POWER

Harry S. Truman, President of the United States of America,
To all to whom these Presents shall come, Greeting:
Know Ye That, reposing special trust and confidence in the integrity, prudence, and ability of⋯⋯⋯⋯, Ambassador Extraordinary and Plenipotentiary of the United States of America to the United Kingdom of Great Britain and Northern Ireland, I have invested him with full and all manner of power and authority for and in the name of the United States of

America to meet and confer with any person or persons duly authorized by the Government of the United Kingdom of Great Britain and Northern Ireland, being invested with like power and authority, and with such person or persons to negotiate, conclude, and sign an agreement between the Government of the United States of America and the United Kingdom of Great Britain and Northern Ireland to facilitate the inter-change of patent rights and technical information for defense purposes, together with a related note.

In testimony whereof, I have caused the Seal of the United States of America to be hereunto affixed.

Done at the city of Washington this fifth day of December in the year of our Lord one thousand nine hundred and ········ and of the Independence of the United States of America the one hundred ···········th.

(SEAL)

By the President: (Signed) Harry S. Truman
(Signed) Dean Acheson
   Secretary of State

例　三　十

Vincent Auriol, Président de la République Française, A
toux ceux qui ces présentes Lettres verront, Salut;

Un Accord complémentaire à la Convention générale franco-britannique du 28 janvier 1950, relative aux régimes de sécurité sociale applicables en France et en Irlande du Nord, devant être prochainement signé à Paris, A Ces Causes, Nous confiant entiérement en la capacité, zèle et dévouement de Monsieur ...., Ministre du Travail et de la Sécurité Sociale, et de Monsieur ...., Ministre Plénipotentiaire, Directeur des Affaires Aministratives et Sociales au Ministére des Affaires Etrangères, Nous les avons nommés et constitués Nos Plénipotentiaires à l'effet de négocier, conclure et signer avec le ou les Plénipotentiaires également munis de Pleins Pouvoirs de la part de leur Gouvernement, tels Convention, Déclaration ou Acte quelconque qui seront jugés nécessaires dans l'intérêt de ces Pays.

Promettons d'accomplir et d'exécuter tout ce que Nos dits Plénipotentiaires auront stipulé et signé au nom du Gouvernement de la République Française sans permettre qu'il y soit contrevenu directement ou indirectement ou de quelque manière que ce soit.

En Foi de Quoi, Nous avons fait apposer à ces présentes le Sceau de la République Française.

Fait à Paris, le·············.

(Signed) V. Auriol

Par le Président de la République

(SEAL)   Le Ministre des Affaires Etrangères

(Signed) Schuman

Le Président du Conseil
des Ministres,
(signed) Ant. Pinay

例三十一

領事委任文憑

中華民國總統　為頒給委任文憑事

查在⋯⋯⋯⋯國

地方時有本國人民貿易往來或常川居住稽查保護責任宜專茲有⋯⋯⋯⋯勤

勉誠實特派為中華民國領事駐紮該地所有關係本國人民商務利益及一切事宜均

授給全權俾得依法保護切望

⋯⋯⋯⋯國政府允認奉此委任文憑之⋯⋯⋯⋯為駐⋯⋯⋯領事其執行

領事職務之地區為⋯⋯⋯⋯等地方並予以應享權利與駐在該地之各國領事官毫

無歧異至希推誠協助俾盡厥職為此頒給委任文憑署名蓋章以昭信守須至文憑者

右給駐⋯⋯⋯領事⋯⋯⋯

總統⋯⋯⋯

外交部部長⋯⋯⋯

中華民國　年　月　日　字第　號

領事委任狀（領事委任文憑）
CONSULAR COMMISSION

Chiang Chung-cheng
President of the National Government of
the Republic of China

TO ALL WHO SHALL SEE THESE PRESENTS, GREETING:

Know ye, that reposing special Trust and Confidence in the ability and integrity of Mr.············, I have nominated and appoint him Consul General at············, and do authorize and empower him to have and to hold the said office, and to exercise and to enjoy all the rights, privileges and immunities thereto appertaining, during the pleasure of President of the. Republic of China.

IN TESTIMONY WHEREOF, I have caused these letters to be made patent, and the seal of the Republic of China to be here unto affixed.

Given under my hand, at Nanking, on the············ day of the ············month of the············year of the Republic of China (············, 19············).

(Signed) Chiang Chung-cheng
(Countersigned) ························
Minister of Foreign Affairs .

例 三 十 三

CONSULAR COMMISSION
....

Washington, ...

Excellency:

I have the honor to inform Your Excellency that Mr.······
······, a citizen of the State of ··············, has been appointed
Consul of the United States of America at ············. (in place
of············who formerly held that office.)

In communicating the above information to Your Excellency and enclosing his commission in that capacity, I have
the honor to request that you will be pleased to grant to Mr.
··············the formal exequatur of the Government of His
Majesty············, recognizing him in his consular capacity and
to ask that upon its issurance, you will be pleased to direct
that information thereof be communicated to him, together
with the enclosed commission, at his post of duty.

I avail myself of the occasion to offer to Your Excellency
the assurance of my most distinguished consideration.

Secretary of State
of the United States of America.

Enclosure:

Commission of ············ as Consul of the United States of
America at············.

To His Excellency

The Minister of Foreign Affairs,

....

例 三 十 四

領 事 證 書
EXEQUATUR

中華民國總統　　　　　　　　　　　爲頒給領事證書事

據外交部轉呈

……………國新派駐桀…………………領事官…………委任文憑

請爲察閱准其就職前來本總統准該領事官就任行其職務並准享受

應得之優遇及其特權爲此頒給證書蓋用國璽以昭信守此證

　右給

　　　　　………國駐桀…………領事官…………收執

　　　　　　　　總統………………

　　　　　　　　　外交部部長……………

中　華　民　國…………年…………月………日

例 三 十 五

領 事 證 書
EXEQUATUR
………………………

PRESIDENT OF……………………

TO ALL WHOM IT MAY CONCERN:

Satisfactory evidence having been exhibited to me that
Mr…………. has been appointed Consul of the Republic of
China at…………I do hereby recognize him as such, and declare
him free to exercise and enjoy such functions, powers, and

privileges as are allowed to consular representatives by the Law of Nations or by the Laws of the Republic of ⋯⋯⋯⋯⋯⋯

In testimony whereof, I have caused these Letters to be made Patent, and the Seal of the Republic of⋯⋯⋯⋯⋯to be hereunto affixed.

Done in the City of⋯⋯⋯⋯⋯, this⋯⋯⋯⋯⋯day of⋯⋯⋯⋯A.D.
One thousand nine hundred and ⋯⋯⋯⋯⋯⋯ and of the INDEPENDENCE OF⋯⋯⋯⋯⋯⋯, the.⋯⋯⋯⋯⋯.

(sgd) ⋯⋯⋯⋯⋯⋯⋯⋯⋯⋯⋯⋯⋯⋯

By the President:
(sgd)⋯⋯⋯⋯⋯⋯⋯⋯⋯⋯
Secretary of Foreign Affairs

例 三 十 六

領 事 證 書

EXEQUATUR

His Majesty's Principal Secretary of State for Foreign Affairs presents his compliments to the Chinese Ambassador and with reference to His Excellency's note No. ⋯⋯⋯⋯⋯of the 15th of January respecting the appointment of Mr.⋯⋯⋯⋯⋯ as Consul-General of China at⋯⋯⋯⋯⋯, has the honour to state that The King's Exequatur empowering this gentleman to act in his official capacity received His Majesty's signature on the 1st March.

Foreign Office, S.W.I.

七、慶　　賀
Congratulatory Messages

友邦國慶，或元首及外交部長等就職，或其他慶典，本國元首及外交部長照例發電或行文申賀，對方亦囘電或復文答謝。此項文字雖係例行，但不可疏忽。

茲分國慶，獨立，就職及其他（包括慶賀新年，抗戰勝利，廢除領事裁判權，謝賀壽誕，解決重大問題及其他種種）各節，分別舉例如次：

國　　慶
National Anniversary

例　　一

His Excellency Lin Sen

....

In the name of the Government and people of the United States I extend to Your Excellency cordial felicitations and sincere best wishes upon the National Anniversary.

F. D. Roosevelt

復　　電

His Excellency
Franklin D. Roosevelt

....

In the name of the Government and people of China I heartily thank you and the American people for your most welcome message of congratulation on the occasion of the National Anniversary of the Republic.

Lin Sen

His Excellency President··········
Mexico City, Mexico.

On this happy occasion of your Independence Day, I take great pleasure in extending to Your Excellency my sincerest felicitations and best wishes for Your Excellency's personal welfare and the prosperity of Mexico.

Chiang Kai-shek
President of the Republic of China

His Excellency ··············
President of Executive Yuan
Republic of China

On behalf of His Majesty's Government, I wish to thank Your Excellency and the Chinese Government for congratulatory message on the occasion of Thai National Day, and I desire to take this opportunity to convey to Your Excellency my sincere good wishes for your personal welfare and the continued prosperity of the Republic of China.

····················
President of the Council
of Ministers of Thailand

例 四

To Prime Minister Mr. Constantine Caramanlis:

On the occasion of the anniversary of the Independence of Greece, declared 139 years ago at Aghia Lavra, may I extend to you and the people of Greece the warmest congratulations of my Government and of the people of the United States of America.

We know the pride with which you and your country-men view the freedom which was declared on that great occasion and which has been so stalwartly defended ever since.

On behalf of my Government and its people I take this opportunity to reaffirm our confidence in the continuing friendship which exists between our two countries and our two peoples.

Chargé d'affairs
American Embassy in Greece

例 五

His Excellency Dr.············
President of the Republic of Colombia
Bogota

On the occasion of National Day of the Republic of Colombia, I wish to extend to Your Excellency and through You to the Colombian Government and people my hearty congratulations and sincere wishes for Your personal well-being and the prosperity of Your nation.

Chiang Kai-shek

獨　　立

Independence

例　　一

PLAIN

HIS EXCELLENCY THE MINISTER FOR FOREIGN AFFAIRS
GOVERNMENT OF ROYAL KINGDOM OF LIBYA
TRIPOLI (Please forward to Bengasi if necessary)

ON BEHALF OF THE GOVERNMENT OF THE
REPUBLIC OF CHINA, I AM HAPPY TO EXTEND TO
YOUR EXCELLENCY MY SINCERE CONGRATULATIONS
ON THE SOLEMN OCCASION OF THE PROCLAMATION
OF THE INDEPENDENCE OF LIBYA. I AVAIL MYSELF
OF THIS OPPORTUNITY TO CONVEY TO YOUR EXCEL-
LENCY MY BEST WISHES FOR YOUR PERSONAL WELL-
BEING AND SUCCESS AND PROSPERITY OF YOUR
NATION.
SIGNED ················, MINISTER FOR FOREIGN AFFAIRS
OF THE REPUBLIC OF CHINA

例　　二

Archbishop Makarios
Nicosia

I heartily congratulate you on your election as first
President of the Cyprus State. My personal and my people's
wishes will accompany you in your untiring efforts for the
prosperity and progress of independent Cyprus.

King Paul

Archbishop Makarios

Cyprus

Please accept my sincere congratulations on your proclamation as President-elect. I recognise the Cypriot people's attachment to the principles of democracy, freedom, justice and peace. I am confident Cyprus will take its honoured place among the free nations of the world.

President Eisenhower

Congolese Premier

On the occasion of the proclamation of the independence of the Congo, I wish to express to Your Excellency the warmest congratulations of the Hellenic Government and the Greek people and their sincerest good wishes for the prosperity of the new State. Our compatriots are happy to be able to contribute by their labour in complete harmony with the Congolese people whose aspirations towards progress in peace and security they share.

C. Karamanlis

Premier of Greece

就　　職
Assumption of Office

例　　一

His Excellency

President Roosevelt

Whitehouse, Washington D.C.

On behalf of the National Government and Chinese people I tender to Your Excellency our heartiest congratulations upon your inauguration and sincerely hope that the friendly relations so happily existing between our two Republics will be further strengthened during your administration.

LIN SEN

復　　電

His Excellency Lin Sen

President of the National Government

of the Republic of China

Nanking.

I am sincerely grateful for your Excellency's courteous felicitation on the occasion of the assumption of my official duties and am happy to extend on behalf of the American Government and people and in my own name reciprocal greetings and good wishes.

Franklin D. Roosevelt

例　　二

To the President of the Republic of Turkey:

On behalf of the Chinese Government and People, I send to Your Excellency my heartiest congratulations upon your ascension to the Presidency of the Republic of Turkey and my most sincere wishes for the welfare and prosperity of your great country and people.

Lin Sen

復　　電

President Lin Sen:

I am sincerely grateful for Your Excellency's most cordial felicitations on the occasion of my assumption of office as President of Turkey and desire to extend on behalf of the Government and people of Turkey to Your Excellency our reciprocal greetings and good wishes.

Turkish President

例　　三

His Majesty the King of Greece
Athens

On behalf of the Chinese Government and people, I desire to send to Your Majesty my heartiest congratulations upon Your ascension to the Throne as King of Greece and my sincere good wishes for the welfare and prosperity of your country and people.

Lin Sen

復　　電

President Lin Sen

I greatly appreciatee Your Excellency's most courteous felicitations upon my ascension to the Throne as King of Greece and wish to extend to Your Excellency our reciprocal greetings and sincere good wishes.

King Paul

例　　四

HIS EXCELLENCY
THE PRESIDENT OF THE CHINESE REPUBLIC
TAIPEI

ON THE OCCASION OF THE RE-ELECTION OF YOUR EXCELLENCY AS PRESIDENT OF THE REPUBLIC OF CHINA I SEND YOU MY SINCERE CONGRATULATIONS AND WARM WISHES FOR YOUR PERSONAL HAPPINESS AND FOR THE PROSPERITY OF THE GALLANT CHINESE NATION.

PAUL R.

復　　電

I AM DEEPLY APPRECIATIVE OF THE CORDIAL MESSAGE YOU SENT ME ON THE OCCASION OF MY INAUGURATION STOP PLEASE ACCEPT MY BEST WISHES FOR YOUR MAJESTY'S PERSONAL WELLBEING AND PROSPERITY OF YOUR NATION.

CHIANG KAI-SHEK
PRESIDENT OF THE REPUBLIC OF CHINA

Excellency,

I wish to thank you for your letter of the 5th instant, by which you were good enough to inform me of the reelection Their Excellencies President Chiang Kai-shek and Vice President Chen Cheng to the respective posts of the Republic of China and to ask you to convey to them my congratulations.

I avail myself of this opportunity to renew to Your Excellency the assurances of my highest consideration.

Constantine Karamanlis

Excellency,

I have the honour to inform Your Excellency that I had received yesterday a wire requesting me to convey to you the thanks of Their Excellencies President Chiang Kai-shek and Vice President Chen Cheng for your congratulations on their re-election to the Presidency and Vice Presidency of the Republic of China.

Please accept, Your Excellency, the assurances of my highest consideration.

Chinese Ambassador

His Excellency

  Mr.················

  Prime Minister

    ···················

Monsieur le Ministre,

Me référant à ma lettre No. ⋯⋯⋯⋯du ⋯⋯⋯⋯, j'ai l'honneur de porter à la connaissance de Votre Excellence que le Général Chiang Kai-shek qui avait été réélu Président de la République par l'assemblée Nationale en date du 22 Mars 1954, inaugurera son second mandat présidential le 20 Mai 1954, au cours d'une cérémonie solennelle à laquelle assisteront les membres des Missions Diplomatiques Etrangères à Taipei, des Délégations Spéciales de pays amis et des Représentants de diverses Organisations Civiques Chinoises.

Veuillez agréer, Monsieur le Ministre, les assurances de ma plus haute considération.

(Signed) Chinese Ambassador

Son Excellence

　Monsieur le Prof. ⋯⋯⋯⋯⋯

　Ministre des Affaires Etrangères

　⋯⋯⋯⋯⋯⋯⋯⋯

復　　　文

Monsieur l'Ambassadeur,

J'ai l'honneur d'accuser réception à Votre Excellence de Sa lettre du ⋯⋯⋯par laquelle Elle a bien voulu me faire part que Son Excellence Monsieur le Général Chiang Kai-shek a été réélu Président de la République par l'Assemblée Nationale en date du 22 Mars 1954 et qu'il inaugurera Son second mandat présidentiel le 20 Mai 1954.

En Vous remerciant de cette aimable communication, je Vous prie d'agréer, Monsieur l'Ambassadeur, les assurances de ma très haute considération.

Turkish Foreign Minister

例　　八

Monsieur le Chargé d'Affaires,

J'ai l'honneur de porter à Votre connaissance que dans le nouveau Cabinet formé par Monsieur·········, j'ai assumé la charge du Ministre des Affaires Etrangères.

Au moment de prendre possession de mes nouvelles fonctions je me plais à espérer que les relations d'amitié et de confiance si heureusement nouées entre votre Honorable Mission et mon éminent prédécesseur continueront, comme par le passé, et je puis vous assurer de l'appui que vous trouverez toujours auprès de moi pour le développement et l'affermissement des rapports amicaux qui existent entre nos deux pays.

Veuillez agréer, Monsieur le Chargé d'Affaires, l'assurance de ma considération distinguée.

復　　文

Monsieur le Ministre,

J'ai l'honneur d'accuser réception à Votre Excellence de Votre obligeante lettre No. ······ en date du 11 courant, par laquelle Vous avez bien voulu m'informer que dans le nouveau Cabinet formé par Son Excellence Monsieur ·········, Vous avez assumé la charge de Ministre des Affaires Etrangères; je remercie bien vivement Votre Excellence de Cette heureuse communication.

Il est certain que sous la haute direction d'une personnalité éminente comme Votre Excellence, les relations d'amitié et de confiance si heureusement nouées entre Votre illustre prédécesseur et ma Mission, continueront comme par le passé, et de ma part, étant déjà honoré de l'appui bienveillant et de

l'amitié personnelle de Votre Excellence, je puis Vous assurer
que Vous trouverez en ma modeste personne un fidèle colla-
borateur pour le développement et l'affermissement des rapports
amicaux qui existent entre nos deux pays frères.

Veuillez agréer, Monsieur le Ministre, les assurances de
ma plus haute considération.

例　　　九

To President Garcia

Manila

On behalf of the Government and people of the Republic
of China I wish to extend to Your Excellency our heartfelt
congratulations upon your succession to the presidency of the
Republic of the Philippines, while deeply mourning the passing
away of President Magsaysay. We find consolation in the fact
that your great predecessor is succeeded by such an eminent
statesman as Your Excellency. We are fully confident that
the traditional friendship between our two countries will be
maintained and further promoted under your administration
I avail myself of this opportunity to convey to Your Excellency
my best wishes for your personal welfare and the prosperity
of your nation.

Chiang Kai–shek

President of the Republic

of China

To President.....................

....

Upon your receiving a new mandate of the people of the Philippines I extend to you my warmest congratulations. I feel sure that the traditional ties of friendship between our two countries will be further strengthened. Best wishes for your continuing success.

....

To the Secretary of Foreign Affairs
　of.................

Heartiest congratulations on your appointment as Secretary of Foreign Affairs of the Republic of.........and best wishes for every success. I am happy to have the privilege of continuing to work with Your Excellency for the close cooperation between our two countries.

....

Minister of Foreign Affairs
Republic of China

Mr. John Kennedy,

On the day of your taking charge of the high office of President of the United States of America, I wish to convey to you again the warmest congratulations of the Royal Government and myself personally.

The progress of the American Nation, the defence of Liberty and the safeguard of Peace constitute the heavy burden you are shouldering today. I wish you the fullest success.

In your task you are followed by the goodwill and hope of the free world and of the Greek people, in particular, whom close ties of friendship and gratitude unite with your great country.

Greek Prime Minister

例 十 三

....

Dear Mr. Prime Minister,

On behalf of my Government and myself, please accept my warmest and most sincere congratulations on your over-whelming victory at the General Election on···········May I also say that your victory is a victory of the Free World.

During the past six years that you have been Prime Minister, I have witnessed an all-round improvement in the economic, social and political life of···········I am sure that I can look forward to still greater successes of your Government in the future.

Please accept, dear Mr. Prime Minister, the assurances of my highest consideration.

(Signed) ·······················

His Excellency

  Mr.·····················

    Prime Minister

     ··············

Monsieur le Ministre,

J'ai l'honneur d'accuser réception de la lettre de Votre Excellence datée du ···········par laquelle Vous avez bien voulu porter à ma connaissance que Vous avez assumé le portefeuille des Affaires Etrangères dans le nouveau Gouvernement qui a prêté serment le ···········sous le Présidence de Son Excellence Monsieur···········.

Tout en présentant mes plus sincères félicitations à Votre Excellence, je me réjouis de l'occasion qui me sera ainsi donnée de poursuivre les agréables relations officielles que j'entretenais avec Votre Excellence, dans le même esprit de compréhension mutuelle qui les caractérisait dans le passé.

Je saisis cette occasion, Monsieur le Ministre, pour renouveler à Votre Excellence les assurances de ma plus haute considération.

Chinese Ambassador

Son Excellence

Monsieur·····················

Ministre des Affairs Etrangères

En ville.

The Chief of Protocol presents his compliments to Their Excellencies and Messieurs the Chiefs of Mission and has the honor to inform that the Honorable ············, Permanent Representative of ·········· to the United Nations, was today appointed and has assumed his duties as Acting Secretary of Foreign Affairs, vice the Honorable············, resigned.

<h1 style="text-align: center">復　　文</h1>

The Ambassador of the Republic of China presents his compliments to the Chief of Protocol of the Department of Foreign Affairs and has the honor to acknowledge the receipt of the latter's memorandum of·········· informing that The Honorable···········, Permanent Representative of···········to the United Nations, was appointed on············and has assumed his duties as Acting Secretary of Foreign Affairs, vice the Honorable···········, resigned.

The Ambassador of the Republic of China wishes to thank the Chief of Protocol for this information and avails himself of this opportunity to extend to His Excellency········· his sincere felicitations and best wishes for his success.

<h1 style="text-align: center">其　　他</h1>
Miscellaneous

<h2 style="text-align: center">例　　一</h2>

TO THE CHINESE GOVERNMENT:

I WISH TO CONVEY TO YOU AND THE PEOPLE OF CHINA THE WARM GOOD WISHES THE GOVERNMENT AND PEOPLE OF CANADA FOR THE CHRISTMAS SEASON AND THE NEW YEAR OUR PURPOSE OUR THOUGHTS AND OUR EFFORTS ARE ONE WITH YOURS IN THE DETERMINATION TO DO IN OUR POWER TO DEFEND PRESERVE AND RESTORE FREEDOM THROUGHOUT THE WORLD.

DEPARTMENT OF EXTERNAL AFFAIRS

DEPARTMENT OF EXTERNAL AFFAIRS
OTTAWA

FOLLOWING FROM GENERALISSIMO CHIANG KAI-
SHEK IN REPLY TO THE RIGHT HONOURABLE WL
MACKENZIE KING'S MESSAGE (QUOTE) IN THE NAME
OF THE GOVERNMENT AND PEOPLE OF CHINA I THANK
YOU MOST SINCERELY FOR YOUR COURTEOUS MES-
SAGE AND THE KIND SENTIMENTS WHEREIN EXPRESS-
ED WHICH I WISH TO RECIPROCATE (STOP) IT IS OUR
UNSWERVING DETERMINATION TO CONTRIBUTE OUR
EFFORTS AS WE HAVE BEEN DOING IN CONCERT WITH
ALL ALLIED NATIONS TOWARDS THE CONSUMATION
OF OUR SUPREME COMMON CAUSE OF JUSTICE AND
HUMAN DECENCY (UNQUOTE)

MINISTRY OF FOREIGN AFFAIRS

例　　　二

Waichiaopu, Chungking

Please submit to Generalissimo Chiang Kai-Shek following message from Sir⋯⋯⋯⋯: "Your most kind telegram of good wishes arrived just as I was about to send you all my very best wishes and congratulations upon glorious ending of your long drawn-out war. My heart goes out to you and all people of China that their long suffering is over. May they now devote all their incomparable energies to task of reconstruction of their country as great leader in democracy in Far East. ⋯ ⋯⋯⋯⋯" Koo

Chinese Embassy
London

Forward Following message to Sir ·········· Quote Many thanks for your telegram of congratulation upon the defeat of Japan. I appreciate very much your good wishes on this day of victory as I always did your sympathy with China. Now that the war is over, the Chinese people and government are determined to redouble efforts not only for the consummation of the task of national reconstruction but also for the building of a just and lasting peace in cooperation with their allies.

Chiang Kai-shek

例　　三

His Excellency
　　Dr.·····················
　　Chinese Minister for Foreign Affairs

On the occasion of the signing of the treaty between our two countries for the relinguishment of extraterritorial rights in China, I wish to send to you my cordial greetings and warmest congratulations on the successful outcome of these negotiations. The agreement now reached sets the seal on the bond of friendship which has already been signed in the blood of those both British and Chinese who are fighting to end aggression. In perfect equality of rights our two free peoples now stand side by side together with the other United Nations as the champions in war and the guarantors when peace is assured of a world in which East West can live together in freedom, prosperity and peace.

·····················
Secretary of State for
Foreign Affairs of Great Britain

例　　四

Heartfelt thanks for greeting me on my birthday anniversary and would also like to say that I appreciate your kind thoughts very much. In return please accept my best wishes and kindest regards.

....

例　　五

Dear Mr. President:

The Filipino nation commemorates today the epic stand against aggression taken by the Filipino and American soldiers together at Bataan. Their immortal act of courage has become for us a bright symbol of the firm determination of our two countries to preserve the blessings of freedom and democracy for the world, and of the special friendship that binds our two peoples.

Such a friendship, having been tested in war, cannot be less strong and enduring in peace, moved as our two peoples are to strengthen this relationship in a spirit of sincere understanding, mutual respect and friendly cooperation.

On this the 17th anniversary of Bataan Day, the Filipino people and myself join Your Excellency and the American people in remembering the heroic stand of the soldiers of our two countries in the hallowed fields of Bataan.

Sincerely,

Carlos P. Garcia

復　　文

Dear Mr. President:

On the 17th anniversary of Bataan, a campaign of heroic memory, I extend best wishes to you and to the people of the Philippines on behalf of the people of the United States.

The bonds of brotherhood forged in the gallant defense of Bataan and Corregidor are part of the tradition which unites our two countries. Our continuing efforts to defend and encourage the growth of democratic institutions throughout the world is a corollary of this tradition in this campaign, we will together press on to win the victory, peace with honor and progress for mankind.

It is a privilege to join you in commemorating the indomitable spirit of Bataan.

Sincerely,
Dwight D. Eisenhower

例　　六

Monsieur le Ministre,

J'ai l'honneur de faire part à Votre Excellence de la joie profonde avec lequelle j'ai salué le règlement de la question de Chypre, règlement dans lequel Vous avez joué un rôle prépondérant.

Qu'il me soit permis d'adresser à Votre Excellence mes félicitations les plus chaleureuses pour le courage, l'opiniâtreté et l'énergie que vous avez manifestés et qui ont fini par mener à l'aboutissement des pourparlers, et au succès de Votre mandat.

J'espère fermement que le peuple cypriote, si durement
éprouvé, connaitra dorénavant une ère de paix et de prospérité
et qu'il pourra, dans la tranquillité, se livrer à son oeuvre de
progrès et de reconstruction.

Je saisis cette occasion, Monsieur le Ministre, pour
renouveler à Votre Excellence les assurances de ma très haute
considération.

....

Son Excellence
M.·····················
Ministre des Affaires Etrangères
En Ville.

例　　七

....

Dear Mr. President:

I am happy to avail myself of the opportunity of Ambas-
sador···········'s return to···········to convey to you my sincere
greetings.

China and···········are close neighbors. We were allies and
comrades-in-arms in war. We are joined today in our common
struggle against the Communist menace.

I am deeply gratified to learn of the phenomenal success
of your fight against the Communist movement as well as the
great progress which your country has achieved in agriculture
and industry and in the improvement of the economic and
cultural well-being of your people. Your great country has
become a shining example of how an Asian country can attain

economic development in an atmosphere of freedom and democracy.

With best wishes and regards,

Sincerely yours,

....

His Excellency··············

President of the··············

....

復　　　函

....

Dear Mr. President

It is a great pleasure to receive your kind message of ·············.

Your observations about the progress of my country in the suppression of the communist movement and the promotion of the economic well–being of the people are most encouraging.

Bound together by a common political ideology and faced by a common threat of aggression and subversion, China and ·········will continue to stand united in all efforts to strengthen their positions against the advance of communism.

With my warm personal regards. I am

Sincerely yours,

....

His Excellency

....

President of the Republic of China

....

例　　八

Monsieur le Grand Maréchal,

De retour ce matin de mon voyage à············, j'ai l'honneur de prier Votre Excellence de bien vouloir transmettre à la Famille Royale les respectueuses félicitations du Corps Diplomatique ainsi que les miennes propres pour la brillante victoire remportée par Son Altesse Royale le Prince Héritier aux Jeux Olympiques de Rome.

Cette victoire dont le retentissement a été mondial a été vivement ressentie par nous tous et je me fais l'interprète de tous mes Collègues en assurant Leurs Majestés de l'mmense joie que nous avons tous éprouvée.

Je saisis cette occasion, Monsieur le Grand Maréchal, pour renouveler à Votre Excellence les assurances de ma très haute considération.

復　　函

Monsieur l'Ambassadeur,

En réponse à votre lettre du············courant, j'ai l'honneur de transmettre à Votre Excellence, ainsi qu'aux membres du Corps Diplomatique, les remerciements très sincères de Leurs Majestés pour vos félicitations adressées au Prince Royal pour son triomphe aux Jeux Olympiques.

Veuillez agréer, Excellence, l'expression de ma très haute .considération

Grand Maréchal de la Cour.

例　九

Monsieur le Doyen,

J'ai l'honneur de porter à la connaissance de Votre Excellence que le 9 Avril prochain sera célébré à Luxembourg le mariage de L. L. A. R. le Prince············de Luxembourg et la Princesse············de Belgique.

Ce Jour-la, un régistre sera ouvert à la Légation pour les membres du Corps diplomatique et les notables qui désireraient présenter leurs félicitations. Ce régistre sera ouvert de 10 heures à 13 h et de 15 h à 18 heures.

Je vous serais reconnaissant de bien vouloir, en votre qualité de Doyen, faire part de ce qui précède aux missions diplomatiques,

Veuillez agréer, Monsieur le Doyen, les assurances de ma haute considération.

(Signed) Minister of Belgium

八、悼　　慰
Condolences

　　凡遇友邦元首及重要官員死亡或發生其他不幸事件，本國元首，有關官員或駐在地使節必須拍發電文。表示悼唁及慰問之意。通告死亡之文件，公文紙均加印黑色粗邊。

　　本節舉例從例一至例二十二為悼唁死亡之文電，從例二十三至例二十六為電慰其他不幸事件。

例　　一

January 24, 1965

Lady Churchill
28 Hude Park Gate
LONDON

　　We realize that the passing of Sir Winston leaves a void which no words of sympathy can fill, but we hope that the knowledge of the respect, admiration and affection with which he is universally held will in time assuage your sorrow. History will record him as a dedicated patriot who saved his country in her darkest hours during World War II, and one of the outstanding world leaders, for indeed his was a life resplendent with courage, resourcefulness and resoluteness. We salute the memory of a great statesman and a valiant warrior. To you, his life companion who contributed so much and so long to his happiness and success, and to all members of your family, we would like to express our heartfelt condolences.

Chiang Kai-shek and Chiang Soong Mayling.

President Garcia
Manila

I am deeply grieved at the national loss the Republic of the Philippines has sustained in the tragic passing of your great President His Excellency Ramon Magsaysay. I hasten to extend to Your Excellency and to the people of the Philippines an expression of the profound sorrow and sympathy felt by the government and people of the Republic of China, President Magsaysay's devoted service to his own country and his great contribution to the cause of the free world will be long remembered not only by the people of the Philippines but also by peoples all over the world. Please convey to Mrs. Magsaysay on behalf of Madame Chiang and myself our deep personal sympathy and condolences in their bereavement.

Chiang Kai–shek

復　　　文

His Excellency
　Chiang Kai–shek
　　President of the Republic of China

I acknowledge with deep appreciation Your Excellency's message of March 18, 1957, expressing your grief on the tragic passing of our beloved President Ramon Magsaysay. Such expression of sympathy would no doubt alleviate our sorrows.

On behalf, therefore, of the people and Government of the Philippines and of the family of the late President, as well as on my own, please accept my most sincere appreciation for your kind words of sympathy.

(SGD.) CARLOS P. GARCIA
President of the Philippines

例　　三

My dear President:

I have received instructions from the Prime Minister of the United Kingdom of Great Britain and Northern Ireland, Mr. Harold Macmillan, P. C. M. P., to convey to Your Excellency the following personal message:

"My colleagues and I have been deeply shocked to hear the tragic news of the death of President Magsaysay.

Through this sad accident the Philippine people have lost a well-beloved patriot and fighter for liberty. As friends and allies the people of the United Kingdom join with the Philippine people in mourning their loss and on the behalf of Her Majesty's government I wish to convey heartfelt condolences to all those bereaved."

Believe me, my dear Mr. President,

Yours sincerely,

(sgd.) British Ambassador

例　　四

To the Secretary of Foreign Affairs
Manila
Sir,

I have the honour to request that you be good enough to convey to the Government of the Philippines, on behalf of myself and the whole staff of Her Majesty's Embassy, our profound sorrow on the tragic death of the late President Ramon Magsaysay. His death in the prime of his life is a grievous loss to the Philippine people and it will be mourned throughout the free world where his qualities as a national leader and a champion of freedom and justice had placed him in a pre-eminent position.

I am sure, however, that though his mortal life is now ended his spirit will live on among his people to cherish and foster the ideals of which while living he was so stalwart a champion.

I would also be grateful if a message of our deepest sympathy might be conveyed to Mrs. Magsaysay and her children in the terrible loss which they are called upon to bear.

I have the honor to be,

Sir.

Your obedient servant,

....

H. B. M. Ambassador

例　　　五

The Hon. Carlos P. Garcia
President of the Philippines
Manila

We are profoundly shocked and grieved at the tragic news of the sudden death of President Magsaysay and his fellow ministers. The Royal Hellenic Government and the people of Greece wish to express to the government and the people of the Philippines as well as to the families of the deceased in particular their deep sympathy in their bereavement.

Evanghelos Averoff–Tossizza
Minister for Foreign Affairs
of Greece

Monsieur le Ministre,

J'ai le plus douloureux devoir de vous annoncer le décès de Sa Majesté le Roi Fuad I, mon Auguste Souverain, survenu le 28 avril à 13h. 30.

En portant cette triste nouvelle à la connaissance de Votre Excellence, je saisis l'occasion de vous renouveler l'assurance de la très haute considération.

(signature)

例　　七

....

Monsieur le Chargé d'Affaires,

J'ai le profond regret de vous annoncer le décès de Sa Majesté le Roi Haakon VII de Norvège, survenu à Oslo ce matin.

Un régistre de condoléances sera ouvert à cette Légation, No. 8,··········, jusqu'au 27 septembre···········.

Veuillez agréer, Monsieur le Chargé d'Affaires, les assurances de ma considération la plus distinguée.

(signed by the Minister)

例　　　八

NOTE VETBALE

L'Ambassadeur d'Italie présente ses compliments aux Chefs de Mission accrédités à..............et a l'honneur de les informer, dans sa qualité de Doyen temporaire du Corps Diplomatique, qu'à l'occasion du décès de Sa Majesté le Roi Haakon de Norvège, Sa Majesté le Roi des Hellènes a fixé un Deuil de Cour de la durée de quinze jours à partir du 21 septembre jusqu'au 5 octobre y compris.

La Légation dè Norvège d'autre part informe qu'un registre des condoléances est ouvert auprès de la Légation jusqu'au 27 septembre············.

L'Ambassadeur d'Italie saisit cette occasion pour renouveler aux Chefs de Mission accrédités à············les assurances de sa très haute considération.

　　　　..........................

AUX CHEFS DE MISSION ACCREDITES A·········
EN VILLE

例　　　九

Excellency,

I have the honour to inform you with deep regret of the death on March 24 of Her Majesty Queen Mary.

The Embassy will be open for the expression of condolences from 10 a.m. to 12 noon and from 2 p.m. to 5 p.m. on March 26 and March 27.

Accept, Excellency, the renewed assurances of my highest consideration.

(SGN.) Canadian Ambassador

復　　文

Monsieur l'Ambassadeur,

J'ai l'honneur, Excellence, d'accuser réception de la lettre que Vous avez bien voulu m'adresser en date du············ pour me faire part du décès de Sa Majesté la Reine Mary, survenu le 24 Mars 1953.

Je tiens à exprimer à Votre Excellence, en ma qualité de Doyen du Corps Diplomatique à ············ et à titre personnel, mes sympathies les plus sincères pour le deuil qui vient de frapper Votre Pays.

Je me suis associé très volontiers à l'hommage rendu à la Mémoire de Sa Majesté la Reine Mary en signant le registre expose à l'Ambassade du Canada.

Veuillez agréer, Monsieur l'Ambassadeur, les assurances de ma très haute considération.

Son Excellence

Monsieur··················

Ambassadeur du Canada.

··················

復　　文

Monsieur l'Ambassadeur,

J'ai l'honneur d'accuser réception de la lettre du 27 mars par laquelle Votre Excellence a bien voulu m'offrir ses condoléances à l'occasion du décès de Sa Majesté la Reine Marie, survenu le 24 mars et je tiens à Vous exprimer mes sincères remerciements.

Veuillez agréer, Monsieur l'Ambassadeur, l'assurance de ma très haute considération

Your Excellency,

It is with regret that I have to inform you of the death in Cape Town on the...............of the Honourable..............., Prime Minister of the Union of South Africa.

A Memorial Service will be held in Cape Town on Wednesday the 27th. and the interment will take place in Pretoria on Saturday the 30th.

A register will be open at the Legation between 10 a.m. and 1 p.m. on Wednesday the 27th.

Please accept, Your Excellency, the renewed assurance of my highest consideration.

(Signed) ·······················

例　十　一

Le Ministère des Affaires Etrangères a le très vif regret de porter à la connaissance de Leurs Excellences Messieurs les Chefs des Missions que le Président de la République ······ ······est décédé le 10 Novembre à 9h. 05 du matin.

Il a l'honneur de les informer que Monsieur·········,Président de la Grande Assemblée Nationale de Turquie a assumé, en vertu de l'Article 33 de la Loi d'Organisation Constitutionnelle l'intérimat de la Présidence de la République.

·······························

La Légation de Chine a l'honneur d'accuser réception avec l'émotion douloureuse, au Ministère des Affaires Etrangéres de la Rèpublique⋯⋯⋯, de Sa note No⋯⋯⋯en date du⋯⋯⋯, par laquelle Il a bien voulu l'informer de la triste nouvelle de la perte cruelle pour la grande Nation⋯⋯⋯, dans la personne de Son Excellence, l'illustre Président de la République,⋯⋯⋯

Cette Légation s'empresse de L'informer que son Gouvernement et la nation chinoise qui la considérent comme une grande perte de toute l'Asie, partagent avec la plus profonde sympathie, le dueil national et la douleur immense de la noble Nation soeur, et elle s'associe toute entière avec l'égale douleur, à toutes les manifestations de sympathie et à toutes les cérémonies funébres à la mémoire du grand chef génial de la ⋯⋯⋯nouvelle.

⋯⋯⋯⋯⋯⋯⋯⋯⋯⋯⋯⋯⋯⋯⋯

例　十　二

Monsieur le Ministre,

J'ai l'honneur de transmettre à Votre Excellence, un télégramme que je viens de recevoir de mon Ministre des Affaires Etrangères, Monsieur Wang Chung-hui, à la triste occasion de décès de Son Excellence le Président de la République, Atatürk, comme suit:

"Son Excellence, Monsieur Sukru Saracoglu, Ministre des Affaires Etrangères de la République Turque.

Profondément ému de la perte cruelle que la noble Nation Turque soeur vient d'éprouver en la personne du

Prèsident de la Rèpublique, Atatürk, père de la grande
Turquie nouvelle, je m'empresse d'adresser à Votre Excellence, les sincères condoléances de mon Gouvernement et de
la nation chinoise toute entière, ainsi que celles de ma part
personnelle.

Wang Chung–hui"

Veuillez agréer, Monsieur le Ministre, les assurances de
ma plus haute considération.

....

例　十　三

Le Grand Maréchal de la Cour, Grand Maître des Cérémonies, présente ses compliments à Son Excellence le Doyen du
Corps Diplomatique, Ambassadeur de ·········, et a l'honneur
de l'informer qu'à l'occasion du décès de S.A.R. le DUC DE
BRUNSWICK ET LUNEBOURG, Sa Majesté le Roi a fixé un
Deuil de Cour de la durée de dix jours à partir d'aujourd'hui
30 janvier jusqu'au 8 février y compris.

....

復　　文

....

Monsieur le Grand Maréchal de la Cour,

J'ai été profondément affecté par l'annonce de la mort du
père de Sa Majesté la Reine, qui vient de m'être communiquée.

Je prie Votre Excellence de bien vouloir transmettre à Sa
Majesté mes respectueuses condoléances, ainsi que celles de

ma femme et des autres Member de cette Ambassade.

Je saisis cette occasion, Monsieur le Grand Maréchal de la Cour, pour Vous renouveler les assurances de ma très haute considération.

....

Son Excellence
  Monsieur···········
    Grand Maréchal de la Cour
      En Ville.

例　十　四

Sinoembasy
Manila
  Transmit following message from President Chiang to family of late President Quirino:
    "Madame Chiang and I deeply grieved over the passing of former President Elpidio Quirino. Please accept our profound sympathy and sincerest condolences. Chiang Kai-shek"

例　十　五

Excellency:
  It is with profound regret that I perform the duty of informing Your Excellency that His Holiness Pope Pius XII died in Castel Gandolfo this morning October 9th at 10:52 AM.

  I have the honour to add that a Visitors' Book has been opened at the Apostolic Nunciature, 2120, Taft Avenue,·········.

  Accept, Excellency, the renewed assurances of my highest consideration.

Apostolic Nuncio

例 十 六

In behalf of the Filipino people and of myself, I extend heartfelt condolences on the death of·········, former governor-general of the Philippines. A strong friend of the Filipinos and an advocate of Philippine independence,·········was greatly loved by the Filipino people. Long after his term as governor-general, he continued to serve the Philippines as adviser to our Presidents after the grant of independence. In his death the Philippines has lost a great and sincere friend.

例 十 七

Monsieur l'Ambassadeur,

J'ai le profond regret d'annoncer à Votre Excellence le décès de Son Excellence Monsieur ·········, Président Fédéral de la République d'Autriche, survenu subitement l'après-midi du 4 janvier 1957.

Selon la Constitution le Chancelier Fédéral assume les fonctions du défunt jusqu'à l'élection d'un nouveau Président de la République.

Le deuil a été fixé à partir d'aujourd'hui jusqu'au 10 janvier.

Veuillez agréer, Monsieur l'Ambassadeur, les assurances de ma très haute considération.

(SGN.) Ambassadeur d'Autriche

例 十 八

....

IMMEDIATE

Sir,

It is with deep regret that I have the honor to announce to you the death of Her Royal Highness the Princess·············, the elder sister of the King my Sovereign, which took place in London yesterday, the 4th instant, to the great sorrow of His Majesty, the Royal Family and all classes of His Majesty's subjects.

> I have the honour to be,
> With the highest consideration,
> Sir,
> Yours obedient Servant,
> (For the Secretary of State)
> (sd.) ···························

....

例 十 九

The Secretary of Foreign Affairs presents his compliments to Their Excellencies and Messieurs the Chiefs of Mission and has the honor to inform them of the untimely demise of the Honorable············, Under secretary of Foreign Affairs, on······ ······The body of the deceased now lies in state at the············

The Secretary wishes to inform further their Excellencies and Messieurs that the remains of the deceased will be brought to the Cathedral at .... at 7:00 o'clock on Thursday morning, ..., where a Requiem Mass will be held at 8:00 o'clock to which their Excellencies and Messieurs, together with thier ladies, are invited to attend. After the Mass, the remains will be brought to the Department of Foreign Affairs where Necrological Services will be held at its Hall of Flags, at 10:30 o'oclock. The interment will take place in the afternoon of the same day at the La Loma Cemetery. The funeral cortege will leave the Department of Foreign Affairs at 3:00 o'clock in the afternoon.

The Secretary will communicate to the Chiefs of Mission any changes in the funeral services.

例　二　十

Monsieur l'Ambassadeur,

Par la présente lettre j'ai la douleur de porter à la connaissance de Votre Excellence que Madame··········, épouse de Son Excellence le Président de la République Fédérale d'Allemagne, s'est éteinte samedi le 19 juillet 1952 à Bonn.

Le service réligieux aura lieu à Bonn le 23 juillet, l'enterrement le 24 juillet à Stuttgart.

Un régistre de condoléance sera ouvert à cette Ambassade jusqu'au 26 juillet 1952.

Veuillez agréer, Monsieur l'Ambassadeur, les assurances de ma plus haute considération.

(Signed) Chargé d'Affaires

例 二 十 一

Madam,

Only quite recently both my wife and myself have learnt with grief of the death of Your Grandson due to a motor accident in England. Please accept our most sincere condolences

We would like to have called and expressed personally to You, Madam, our heartfelt sympathies in Your bereavement, but we have hesitated to do so because we feel that words seem so empty of meaning before the awful fact of death. To the great silence of the grave, we can only pay a tribute of silence and bow our heads in humility.

Yours most respectfully,
....

Her Royal Imperial Highness
  Princess Nicholas
    ....

例 二 十 二

Chers Monsieur et Madame············,

Ma femme et moi venons d'apprendre le décès de votre fille survenu dans des circonstances particulièrement tragiques.

Nous en avons été terriblement affectés et vous transmettons nos condoléances les plus sincères ainsi que le témoignage de toute notre sympathie.

Veuillez agréer, chers Monsieur et Madame···········, l'assurance de nos sentiments les meilleurs.

To President Prado of Chili,

I have been deeply distressed to learn of the loss of life and damage caused by the avalanche in the district of Ranrahica and send my sincere condolences. Please convey my heartfelt sympathy and that of the Duke of Edinburgh to those who suffered as a result of this catastrophe.

Queen Elizabeth

例 二 十 四

Sur l'instruction de son Gouvernement, la Légation de Chine a l'honneur de transmettre à l'honorable Ministère des Affaires Etrangères de la République Turque, un télégramme adressé au nom du peuple Chinois à Son Excellence Monsieur le Président Ismet Inönü, par l'Association des Relations Etrangères de Chine à⋯⋯⋯⋯et dont le texte est le suivant:

"His Excellency President Ismet Inonu

Chinese people very distressed at destruction caused by earthquake in your great and noble nation. May we extend to Your Excellency and Turkish people our profound sympathy of Chinese people,

Foreign Relations Association
of⋯⋯⋯⋯⋯"

Cette Légation est très obligée à l'Honorable Ministère de vouloir bien faire parvenir le télégramme susmentionné à Sa Haute destination.

⋯⋯⋯⋯⋯⋯⋯⋯

復　文

En réponse à Sa Note Verbale en date du 4 Janvier·········,
le Ministère des Affaires Etrangères a l'honneur d'informer la
Légation de la République Chinoise que le télégrammé de
condoléances adressé à Son Excellence Monsieur le Président
de la République par l'Association des Relations Etrangères de
Chine à ·········· a été transmis à sa Haute Destination et que
le Président de la République, très sensible à ce message,
remercie ladite Association de sa délicate attention.

··

例　二　十　五

Monsieur l'Ambassadeur,

Par lettre du 10 septembre dernier Votre Excellence a
bien voulu me transmettre ses condoléances pour les victimes
des séismes qui ont ravagé les régions d'Orléansville en Algérie.

J'ai été très sensible à cette marque de sympathie et je
tiens à exprimer à Votre Excellence mes très sincères remerciements ainsi qu'aux Membre de l'Ambassade qui se sont
associés à ce témoignage de solidarité.

Je vous prie d'agréer, Monsieur l'Ambassadeur, les
assurances de ma très haute considération./.

(Signed) Ambassador of France

例 二 十 六

Monsieur le Ministre,

J'ai été extrêment affligé par l'annonce des tremblements de terre catastrophiques qui ont ravagé les Iles ················

J'ai l'honneur de prier Votre Excellence, au nom de mon Gouvernement, de bien vouloir recevoir mes condoléances les plus sincères et le témoignage de toute ma sympathie dans cette tragédie qui frappe le peuple grec.

Qu'il me doit permis d'assurer Votre Excellence que le peuple chinois ne manquera pas de ressentir une profonde douleur en apprenant les souffrances que traverse la Nation Amie.

Je Vous prie de bien vouloir agréer, Monsieur le Ministre, les assurances de ma très haute considération.

(Signed) ·····················

Son Excellence

Monsieur··············

Ministre des Affairs Etrangères

En Ville.

九、國際會議

International Conferences

今日國際會議事務極繁,除直接間接與聯合國有關之各項會議外,另有各種專門技術性、臨時性及民間組織之種種會議。

我政府自大陸淪陷退處臺灣以後, 我爲維護我在聯合國及各種國際會議中以及國際上之合法地位, 曾不斷與各友邦聯繫合作。我政府爲此類事曾由常駐聯合國代表團, 我駐各國使館或其他途徑洽請友邦或駐在國政府予我積極支助, 會議外交日趨重要, 各使館於正常外交工作之外, 直接間接參與會議外交乃成爲今日新的繁重工作。

例　　一

Excellency,

The keen interest taken in⋯⋯⋯⋯in the peaceful uses of atomic energy has prompted the⋯⋯⋯⋯ Government to submit this year its candidacy for a seat on the Board of Governors of the International Atomic Energy Agency, as I had the honor to inform you by my letter No.⋯⋯⋯⋯, of⋯⋯⋯⋯

In a spirit of cooperation, this candidacy was subsequently withdrawn in order to facilitate the election of Spain.

As, however, the ⋯⋯⋯⋯ Government has a continued interest to participate in the work of said Board of Governors, I have been instructed to inform your Excellency that⋯⋯⋯⋯ will be a candidate for the seat to be vacated by Spain, after its two years' term of service.

It is the earnest hope of the⋯⋯⋯⋯Government that your Government will be in a position to lend its valuable support to the above candidacy.

Please accept, Excellency, the renewed assurances of my highest consideration.

....

Permanent Representative of·············
to the United Nations.

H.E.·····················

Permanent Representative of············
to the United Nations
New York

復　　　文

....

Excellency,

I have the honor to acknowledge receipt of your note dated············, informing me of the decision of the ··············· Government to seek election to the Board of Governors of the International Atomic Energy Agency, to succeed Spain after its two years' term of service.

I have the honor to inform Your Excellency that the contents of your note have been transmitted to my Government which will no doubt give the matter its most careful consideration.

Please accept, Excellency, the renewed assurances of my highest consideration.

....

Permanent Representative of··············
to the United Nations

H.E. Mr.·····················

Permanent Representative of············
to the United Nations
New York

復　　文

Excellency:

　　With reference to my letter dated⋯⋯⋯⋯(Ref. No.⋯⋯⋯⋯)
concerning the decision of the ⋯⋯⋯⋯ Government to seek
election to the Board of the Governors of the International
Atomic Energy Agency, I have been instructed to inform Your
Excellency that the ⋯⋯⋯⋯ Government will be happy to
support the candidature of ⋯⋯⋯⋯ for a seat on the Board
of Governors of the International Atomic Energy Agency
during the Fifth Regular Session of the General Conference of
the Agency and that the⋯⋯⋯⋯ Delegation will be instructed
to vote accordingly.

　　Accept, Excellency, the renewed assurances of my highest
consideration.

⋯⋯⋯⋯⋯⋯⋯⋯⋯⋯⋯
Permanent Representative of⋯⋯⋯⋯
to the United Nations.

例　　　二

　　The Embassy of the Republic of ⋯⋯⋯⋯ presents its
compliments to the Department of Foreign Affairs of the⋯⋯⋯
⋯⋯and, with reference to the latter's memorandum of⋯⋯⋯⋯,
Reference No. ⋯⋯⋯⋯, concerning the request of the⋯⋯⋯⋯
Government for support to the candidature of Miss ⋯⋯⋯⋯
for membership in the Commission on the Status of Women
in the United Nations, has the honor to inform the latter that
the Government of the Republic of ⋯⋯⋯⋯ is pleased to give
its full support to the⋯⋯⋯candidate at the elections during the
forthcoming 27th Session of the Economic and Social Council
scheduled to convene in Mexico City from ⋯⋯⋯⋯, and the
⋯⋯⋯⋯delegation to the aforementioned Conference has been
duly instructed to this effect.

　　The Embassy of the Republic of⋯⋯⋯⋯takes this opportunity to renew to the Department of Foreign Affairs of the
⋯⋯⋯⋯the assurances of its highest consideration.

The Embassy of the Republic of .... presents its compliments to the Royal Ministry of Foreign Affairs and has the honor to seek support for a proposed resolution in the forthcoming meeting of the Executive Board of UNESCO scheduled to be held in Paris on the 4th of April relative to the fulfilment of .... 's financial contributions to the said Organization.

Because of financial difficulties beyond its control, the Republic of············had been unable to meet in full its obligations to the Organization in the past few years. With a view to settling its outstanding obligations to UNESCO the Government of the Republic of ············ has decided to make the following proposals:

    1. ....

    2. ....

The············Government hopes that the above proposals will be recommended to the 11th General Conference to be held in November 1960, should they meet first with the approval of the Executive Board.

It will be highly appreciated if the Royal············Government will be kind enough to issue instructions to the············ member of the Executive Board of UNESCO to give his support to the above-mentioned proposals.

The ············ Embassy avails itself of this opportunity to renew to the Royal Ministry of Foreign Affairs the assurances of its highest consideration.

復　　文
NOTE VERBALE

The Royal Ministry of Foreign Affairs present their compliments to the Embassy of the Republic of ·········· and referring to the Note ···········, dated ···········, concerning the reduction of ··········'s contribution to the UNESCO, have the honour to inform the Embassy that instructions have been given to the ·········· Permanent Delegate to the aforesaid Organization to examine the request with sympathy and assist the··········Delegation as far as possible.

The Royal Ministry of Foreign Affairs avail themselves of this opportunity to renew to the Embassy of the Republic of··········the assurances of their highest consideration.

例　　四
NOTE VERBALE

The Ministry of Foreign Affairs present their compliments to the Embassy of the Republic of ·········· and referring to the Note No··········, dated··········, concerning the candidature of··········for the Economic and Social Council of the United Nations have the honour to inform the Embassy that this candidature will be taken into serious consideration.

The Ministry of Foreign Affairs avail themselves of this opportunity to renew to the Embassy of the Republic of ······ ······the assurances of their highest consideration.

例　　五

The Embassy of the Republic of .... presents its compliment to the Department of Foreign Affairs and has the honor to acknowledge receipt of the Department's note, dated ...., ... requesting the support of the .... Government for the candidature of Dr. .... for one of the seats on the Executive Board of the United Nations Educational, Scientific and Cultural Organization (UNESCO).

The Embassy has duly referred the matter to the .... Ministry of Foreign Affairs and, upon the recommendation of the ....Ambassador, the ....Government has agreed to support the candidature of Dr. ....for one of the seats on the Executive Board of the UNESCO in the coming elections which will be held during the Ninth Session of the General Conference to convene on ...., at New Delhi, India.

The .... Delegation to the aforementioned UNESCO Conference will be instructed accordingly to this effect.

例　　六

Excellency:

I have the honor to acknowledge the receipt of Your Excellency's note (Ref: ....) dated ...., ..., informing that the ....Government supported the candidature of Justice ....during the recent elections held for membership to the International Law Commission.

On behalf of the .... Government, I wish to convey our thanks for this kind gesture.

Accept, Excellency, the renewed assurances of my highest consideration.

....
Undersecretary

....

Dear Dr.················

With reference to my informal conversation with you on April 6th, I have just received information from my Government that the United Nations Conference on Food and Agriculture has been postponed and will convene on············, at Hot Springs, Virginia.

The President has approved the following delegates on behalf of the United States:

The Honorable ············, Judge of the United States Court of Claims, Chairman;

....

It is the hope of my Government that the discussions may be as informal as possible and that most of the detailed work will be done in technical sections or committees. Although there will be the usual opening and closing public plenary sessions, it is suggested that the sections and committees might more effectively consider the various topics in executive session. It is planned that the duration of the conference will be determined by the delegation in the light of the progress of the discussions, but at this point it would seem that the conference might be in session for a period of appoximately two weeks.

My Government feels that inasmuch as the Conference will be a technical wartime meeting, there should be an absolute minimum of social entertainment. It is not contemplated that wives or other family members will accompany the delegates. Formal dress will not be necessary, the ordinary business suit being adequate.

For the information of delegates, Hot Springs, the site of Conference, is approximately 290 miles from Washington, D.C., in the State of Virginia. The Homestead Hotel has been reserved for the exclusive use of the Conference and it has facilities for both residential and conference requirements. The Hotel has arranged to grant special rates to the Conference delegations.

Sincerely yours,

(sgn.)⋯⋯⋯⋯⋯⋯⋯⋯⋯⋯

Charge d'Affaires a.i.

例　　八

⋯⋯⋯⋯⋯⋯⋯⋯⋯⋯⋯⋯⋯

My dear Dr.⋯⋯⋯⋯⋯

With reference to my letter of ⋯⋯⋯⋯⋯, with which I transmitted a copy of a telegram from the Secretary of State regarding the proposals of the American Government for a conferance on the limitation of armaments and problems of the Pacific, I beg leave to inform you that the President of the United States desires to fix November 11th as the date of the conference. This date has been accepted by the British Government, and I am directed to ascertain whether this date is agreeable to the Government of China.

I am, dear Dr.⋯⋯⋯⋯⋯,

Very sincerely yours,

(Signed)⋯⋯⋯⋯⋯⋯⋯⋯⋯⋯

His Excellency⋯⋯⋯⋯⋯,

　　Minister for Foreign Affairs.

　　⋯⋯⋯⋯⋯⋯⋯⋯⋯

My dear Mr.⋯⋯⋯⋯:

In reply to your kind letter of yesterday's date informing me that the President of the United States desires to fix November 11th as the date of the Conference on the limitation of Armaments and problems of the Pacific, I have much pleasure in stating that in the view of the Chinese Government the proposed date is an agreeable and appropriate one.

Thanking you to be so good as to transmit the above reply to your Government,

I am, dear Mr.⋯⋯⋯⋯⋯,

Very truly yours,

(Signed) ⋯⋯⋯⋯⋯⋯⋯⋯,

⋯⋯⋯⋯⋯, Esquire,

Charge d'Affaires a.i., etc., etc.,

Legation of the United States

⋯⋯⋯⋯⋯⋯⋯⋯

例　　九

L'Ambassade de ⋯⋯⋯⋯ présente ses compliments au Ministère Royal des Affaires Etrangères et a l'honneur de porter à Sa connaissance qu'une Délégation du Gouvernement de la République de ⋯⋯⋯⋯ assistera à la 12ème Assembleée de l'Organisation Mondiale de la Santé qui aura lieu à Genève à partir du⋯⋯⋯⋯

Il est à présumer que le Bloc Communiste ainsi que leurs sympathisants essayèrent, comme d'habitude, de créer des difficultés à la Delégation··········, notamment en ce qui concerne son droit de représentation à la susdite Assemblée.

L'Ambassade de·········espère que le Ministère Royal des Affaires Etrangères aura l'obligeance de bien vouloir donner les instructions nécessaires à la Délégation ·········· afin que celle-ci s'oppose à toute tentative faite dans ce sens et qu'elle accorde, comme par le passé, son appui à la Délégation·········

L'Ambassade de ·········· saurait gré au Ministère Royal des Affaires Etrangères de bien vouloir lui faire parvenir en réponse à cette Note en temps utile et saisit cette occasion pour lui renouveler les assurances de sa très haue considération.

復　　文

<u>NOTE VERBALE</u>

Le Ministère des Affaires Etrangères présente ses compliments à l'Ambassade de ··········et a l'honneur de porter à sa connaissance, en réponse à sa Note Sub No.·········· en date du 23 avril, que sa demande concernant le droit de représentation du Gouvernement de la République de·········à la 12ème Assemblée de l'Organisation Mondiale de la Santé sera examinée, comme dans le passé, aussi favorablement que possible.

Le Ministère des Affaires Etrangéres saisit cette occasion pour renouveler à l'Ambassade de·········les assurances de sa haute considération.

例　十

L'Ambassade de ⋯⋯⋯⋯ présente ses compliments au Ministère Royal des Affaires Etrangères et a l'honneur de porter à sa connaissance que son Gouvernement vient de lui communiquer que la Délégation ⋯⋯⋯⋯ ne manquera pas d'appuyer la candidature de ⋯⋯à la Commission Administrative et Budgétaire des Nations Unies, lors de la 6ème Assemblée Générale de cet Organisme, en Novembre prochain à Paris.

Etant donné que la Délégation ⋯⋯⋯⋯ compte elle aussi poser de nouveau sa candidature à ladite Commission, l'Ambassade de⋯⋯⋯prie le Ministère Royal des Affaires Etrangères de bien vouloir s'entremettre afin que le Gouvernement Royal ⋯⋯⋯⋯donne les instructions nécessaires à la Délégation Royal ⋯⋯⋯⋯afin que celle-ci appuye de son côté la candidature de la Délégation ⋯⋯⋯⋯

L'Ambassade de⋯⋯⋯⋯saisit cette occasion pour renouveler au Ministère Royal des Affaires Etrangères les assurances de sa très haute considération.

例　十　一

L'Ambassade de ⋯⋯⋯⋯ présente ses compliments au Ministère Royal des Affaires Etrangères et a l'honneur de porter à sa connaissance qu'à la demande de la Délégation permanente⋯⋯⋯à l'O.N.U. le Gouvernement de la République de ⋯⋯⋯⋯ a donné ordre à sa Délégation auprès du Conseil Economique et Social de l'O.N.U. d'appuyer la candidature⋯⋯⋯au dit Conseil.

L'Ambassade de⋯⋯⋯⋯saisit cette occasion pour renouveler au Ministère Royal des Affaires Etrangères les assurances de sa très haute considération.

例　十　二

L'Ambassade de ········· présente ses compliments au Minis-tère Royal des Affaires Etrangères et a l'honneur de porter à Sa connaissance qu'à partir du ············aura lieu à Genéve la Cɔnférence Ordinaire Administrative de la Radio dans le cadre de laquelle il sera precédé à l'élection des Membres du Comité International de l'Enregistrement des Fréquences (International Frequency Registration Board I.F.R.B.).

Le Gouvernement de la République de·········qui est membre de ce Comité, désire poser sa candidature pour sa réelection en vue de continuer à offrir ses services, et cette Ambassade prie le Ministère Royal des Affaires Etrangères de bien vouloir s'entremettre auprès du Gouvernement Royal············ afin que celui–ci donne les instructions nécessaires à sa Délégation pour que celle–ci appuye la candidature du Gouvernement de la République de···········

L'Ambassade de············saurait gré au Ministère Royal des Affaires Etrangères de bien vouloir répondre à cette Note en temps opportun et saisit cette occasion pour lui renouveler les assurances de sa très haute considération.

例　十　三

　　L'Ambassade de ············· présente ses compliments au Ministère Royal des Affaires Etrangères et, en accusant la réception de Sa Note No·············· du ············, par laquelle Il a bien voulu demander à l'Ambassade de solliciter l'appui du Gouvernement de···········à la candidature···········à la Commission de la Condition de la Femme des Nations Unies, a l'honneur de Lui faire savoir que cette Ambassade a transmis immédiatement la dite communication à son Gouvernment et ne manquera pas de communiquer au Ministère Royal la réponse dès sa réception.

　　L'Ambassade de········saisit cette occasion pour renouveler au Ministère Royal des Affaires Etrangères les assurances de sa plus haute considération.

　　　　　　　　　　　　·······························

十、其 他
Other Documents

　　以上本書所論列及舉例之各式各類外交文書,皆平日通用之文牘,茲再將有關抗議, 使館升格,外交團應酬, 簽證與出入境, 索取資料,更換館址等各類文書實例,彙成一節,亦極有用, 其中尤以抗議文書最為重要。凡一方認為對方所作所為, 或一言一動,有損本國之權利者,必須採取行動, 向對方表示抗議。

抗　　議
Protests

例　　一

　　在二次大戰以前, 德國商船在駛離紐約港前其懸掛之德國國旗被美國示威民眾扯下, 德駐美使館臨時代辦奉政府命, 向美國國務院提強硬抗議。國務院亦根據紐約市警察廳報告, 將當時經過情形詳加說明, 茲將此案往來文件錄後。

German Embassy
Washington, July 29, 1935

Mr. Under Secretary of State:

　　By direction of my Government, I have the honor to advise Your Excellency of the following:

　　Late in the evening of July 26, shortly before the departure of the German steamship BREMEN from New York harbor, the German flag flying from the bow of the steamship was violently town off by demonstrators. I am instructed to make the most emphatic protest against this serious insult to the German national emblem, and I venture to express the expectation that everything will be done on the part of the

American authorities charged with the prosecution of criminal offenses in order that the guilty persons may be duly punished.

Accept (etc.).

LEITNER

The Honorable the Acting Secretary of State
Mr. William Phillips
Washington, D.C.

....

復　　文

August 1, 1935.

Sir:

I have received your note of July 29, 1935, in which, upon instructions from your Government, you lodge a protest against the action of demonstrators in New York in tearing down the German flag from the bow of the German steamship BREMEN when that vessel was departing from New York the night of July 26, 1935. You also give expression to the hope that everything will be done by the appropriate American authorities in order that the guilty persons may be punished.

The appropriate authorities in New York have provided me with a full report on this matter, and I enclose a copy for your information. You will note that the police authorities took most extensive precautions in order to prevent any untoward incident; that having learned in advance that a demonstration was planned, they consulted with the representatives of the interested steamship companies and in cooperation with them took all measures which seemed calculated to assure order; and that the incident which actually occurred was in no sense due to neglect on the part of the American authorities.

I invite particular attention to those sections of the report which indicate that a very considerable number of police were detailed to prevent disturbances; that the police suggested measures to prevent persons other than the passengers and other duly authorized visitors from boarding the vessel but that the officers of the steamship line did not deem it necessary to adopt such measures; that unauthorized persons accordingly succeeded in boarding the steamer; that before the vessel sailed such elements started a demonstration; that police authorities took immediate and efficient action with a view to clearing the ship of all unauthorized persons; and that during the course of this action one of the police, namely, Detective Matthew Solomon, in attempting to apprehend the ringleaders, was set upon, knocked down, and sustained serious injury.

I also invite attention to that section of the enclosed report which indicates that the persons implicated in this disorder have been apprehended and are being held for trial.

It is unfortunate that, in spite of the sincere efforts of the police to prevent any disorder whatever, the German national emblem should, during the disturbance which took place, not have received that respect to which it is entitled.

Accept (etc.).

William Phillips

Enclosures:

Report of the New York Police Department, July 29, 1935;
Copy of circular.

Herr Rudolf Leitner

Chargé d'Affaires ad interim of Germany

<h1 style="text-align:center">例　　二</h1>

　　駐在國政府對外國政府及人民因在戰亂時所遭受之意外及不法之
人身及物質上之損害負責賠償。

....

Sir,

　　With reference to the .... Incident which took place
on the .... last year, I have the honour to inform Your
Excellency that, animated by a desire to promote the most
friendly feelings happily subsisting between the......... and the
British people, the Nationalist Government are prepared to
bring about an immediate settlement of the case along the
lines already agreed upon as a result of recent discussions.

　　In the name of the Nationalist Government, I have the
honour to convey in the sincerest manner to His Majesty's
Government in Great Britain their profound regret at the
indignities and injuries inflicted upon the official representatives of His Majesty's Government, the loss of property
sustained by the British Consulate, and the personal injuries
and material damage done to the British residents. Although
it has been found, after investigation of the Incident that it
was entirely instigated by the Communists prior to the
establishment of the Nationalist Government at ...., the
Nationalist Government nevertheless accept the responsibility
therefor.

　　The Nationalist Government have, in pursuance of their
established policy, repeatedly issued orders to the Civil and
Military authorities for the continuous and effective protection
of the life and property of British residents in.........With the
extermination of the Communists and their evil influences

which tended to impair the friendly relations between the ....
.... and British peoples, the Nationalist Government feel
confident that the task of protecting foreigners will henceforth
be rendered easier; and the Nationalist Government undertake
specifically that there will be no similar violence or agitation
against British lives or legitimate interests.

In this connection, I have the pleasure to add that the
troops of the particular division which took part in the unfortunate incident, and the instigation of the Communists, have
been disbanded. The Nationalist Government have in addition
taken effective steps for the punishment of the soldiers and
other persons implicated.

In accordance with the well accepted principles of International Law, the Nationalist Government undertake to make
compensation in full for all personal injuries and material
damage done to the British Consulate and to its officials and
to British residents and their property at··············

The Nationalist Government propose that for that purpose
there be instituted a ········ British joint commission to verify
the actual injuries and damage suffered by the British residents
at the hands of the ··········· concerned, and to assess the
amount of compensation due in each case.

I avail myself of this opportunity to express to Your
Excellency the assurance of my high consideration.

(Signed)······························

His Excellency
　Sir···············
　　His Britannic Majesty's Minister
　　······················

復　　照

....

Sir,

　　I have the honour to acknowledge the receipt of Your Excellency's Note of this day's date which reads as follows:

　　"With reference to the ··········· Incident ··········· and to assess the amount of compensation due in each case."

　　I have also taken note of the orders recently issued by the Nationalist Government regarding the punishment of those implicated and regarding the prevention of similar incidents in the future, and believing that prompt and full effect will be given to the intentions so expressed, I accept on behalf of His Majesty's Government in Great Britain Your Excellency's Note in settlement of the demands contained in the Communication of ··········· 1940, addressed to the former Minister for Foreign Affairs.

　　I avail myself of this opportunity to express to Your Excellency the assurance of my high consideration.

(Signed) For His Majesty's Minister

....

His Excellency

　　Dr.····················

　　Minister for Foreign Affairs

　　.....................

— 195 —

領袖大使代表駐在地外交團為維護外交特權事特備節略向駐在國外交部提出抗議。

The Apostolic Nuncio presents his compliments to His Excellency the Secretary of Foreign Affairs and as Doyen of the Diplomatic Corps has the honor to refer to the events which took place at the chancery of the ………… Embassy in …………on…………, 1958.

The Doyen wishes to inform the Secretary of Foreign Affairs that these events haven't been the subject of discussion by the Chiefs of Mission of the Diplomatic Corps, who have reviewed with care and deliberation all of the Facts Associated with them.

In the first instance, despite assurances to the contrary from the competent authorities, attacks were made on the…… ……Embassy and acts of vandalism, including the desecration of the………… Coat of Arms, and the burning of an effigy of ………… Ambassador, have taken place. During these events, the………Embassy received no adequate protection, as required by all diplomatic custom and practice; furthermore, the authorities appear to have taken no action against those responsible.

The Doyen avails himself of this opportunity to convey, at the unanimous request of the Heads of Mission, their grave concern and formal protest against these happenings.

The diplomatic corps in…………fears that the lack of the provision of customary protection of diplomatic premises on this occasion may again take place, and the Doyen of the Diplomatic Corps takes this opportunity to request from the

Secretary of Foreign Affairs adequate assurances that such breaches of customary and internationally recognized practices will not occur again.

The Doyen of the Diplomatic Corps avails himself of this opportunity of renewing to His Excellency the Secretary of Foreign Affairs the assurance of his highest consideration.

駐在國外交部答覆領袖大使節略

The Secretary of Foreign Affairs presents his compliments to His Excellency the Apostolic Nuncio and Doyen of the Diplomatic Corps and has the honor to acknowledge the receipt of his note dated ··········, referring to the events which took place in the chancery of the··········Embassy in·········· on ···
·········.

The Doyen will remember that on Thursday evening, March the ········, the Secretary had occasion to talk to His Excellency over the telephone and to assure him, that the appropriate ·········· authorities would maintain the dignity of the ·········· Embassy and that adequate protection would be accorded the chancery of the·········Embassy and the residence of the ·········· Ambassador. As a matter of fact, in a press statement issued on the following day, the Secretary deplored the incidents which happened in the chancery and expressed to the········· Ambassador the regrets of the ········· Government therefor. To show the good faith of the ·········· Government, the Secretary even offered to make reparation for any damage which the Embassy might have suffered as a result of the demonstrations. Furthermore, the local authorities are being requested to inquire fully into the case, with a view to ascertaining the responsibility of those involved.

The Secretary is therefore surprised why, despite the foregoing, the Doyen should have sent a protest on behalf of the Diplomatic Corps, and why said note was published in the Press. For this reason, the Secretary will be constrained to allow the publication of this note, in order that the attitude and acts of the ·············· Government may be viewed in the correct perspective.

The ············ Government is always prepared to fulfill its duty of ensuring the enjoyment by the foreign diplomatic missions which have the honor of being accredited to the Republic of the·········of time-honored privileges and immunities. This duty can, however, be better fulfilled if said foreign missions scrupulously and faithfully accord due respect to the laws of the Republic.

The Secretary avails himself of this opportunity to renew to His Excellency the Apostolic Nuncio and Doyen of the Diplomatic Corps the assurances of his highest considerations.

例　　　　四

美駐日大使致日外交部長照會抗議日軍刧掠焚燒美教會財產

Tokyo, ··························

Excellency:

I have the honor to inform Your Excellency that information has reached me through the American Consul at Hanoi, information that has been incontestably substantiated from various sources, to the effect that the mission property of the Christian and missionary Alliance, an American institution, at ··············, was looted on··············, and destroyed by burning on the following day, by Japanese soldiers who were occupying

............The residence of the Reverend ...., the mission's representative, was burned to the ground.

Maps indicating the location of this American property had been transmitted by the American Consulate General at Canton in..........., to the Japanese authorities there. At the time that this looting and burning occurred, the property was stated to have been conspicuously posted with proclamations setting forth its American character and well marked by an American flag. Furthermore, from affidavits executed concerning the affair there appeared to be little doubt that the destruction of the property was deliberate.

I emphatically and most vigorously protest against this patently flagrant violation and destruction of American property. I refer in connection with this act on the part of the agents of the Japanese Government to the repeated assurances given me by the several Ministers for Foreign Affairs of Your Excellency's Government, categorical assurances which were reiterated to me no longer ago than last month during my conversations with Your Excellency's immediate predecessor, that the Japanese Government fully intended to respect American property and American rights and interests in China and had instituted all necessary arrangements toward that end ...What has now transpired with regard to one more American mission property in China is in no way in accord with those expressed assurances.

Your Excellency will undoubtedly appreciate" that the manner of treatment of its property suffered by the American missionary institution in question at the hands of the Japanese military is not one in which my Government and the American people can acquiesce. Military necessity or the exigencies of military operations have been repeatedly put forward in various replies of the Ministry of Foreign Affairs to previous representations concerning cases of this character. In the instance under reference, the facts which are now in hand demonstrate beyond any peradventure that there was no requirement whether military or otherwise which can be interposed to exculpate the responsible Japanese authorities for the destruction and looting of American property.

I reserve the right to claim on behalf of the Christian and Missionary Alliance full compensation for the losses it has sustained. And, in requesting that the Japanese Government cause an immediate investigation to be made of the circumstances described in the foregoing reports, I urge upon Your Excellency that such steps be taken by the Japanese Government as will in fact terminate once and for all any further recurrence of cases such as the present instance.

(Signed) American Ambassador

例　　　五

抗議公司房產暫被軍方佔用

The American Embassy presents its compliments to the Ministry of Foreign Affairs and has the honor to state that it has been informed by the Manager at Chungking of the Standard–Vacuum Oil Company, an American firm, that he has received a letter from the head office of the Company at Shanghai informing him that the company has received a report that the premises occupied by the Company at…………, have been converted by the Chinese military authorities there into a military hospital; the head office in Shanghai instructed the Company's Chungking representative to ask that the American Embassy invite the attention of the Chinese Government to the fact that this step was taken by the Chinese military authorities without consulting the responsible officials of the Standard-Vacuum Oil Company and without having asked for or received the consent of those officials. In these circumstances the Company desires to protest against this measure and to reserve all the rights it possesses in respect of the property in question and articles stored thereon.

The American Embassy, in the light of these statements, reserves on behalf of this American firm the rights to which it is entitled.

Chungking,···············.

例　　六

備　忘　錄

外國使館對駐在國外交部長所作談話提出抗議，
茲將抗議文大要及外交部復文分誌如次：

據聞本月……日，…………外交部長在國會聲稱…………云云，…………國政府駐…………大使館基於本國政府之訓令，認爲遺憾，對此提出抗議。

關於…………，…………政府曾再三向…………政府闡明此項見解，此乃任何人無異議餘地之問題，而……………政府仍繼續提出與…………方面見解相異之主張，斯不得不認爲對…………國之非友好的態度。

復　　文

關於…………大使館奉其本國政府之訓令，就外交部…………部長於本月……日所作……………提出抗議事，大使館……年……月……日備忘錄業經閱悉。

查外交部曾就…………政府對…………問題之一貫立場，迭向大使館闡明在案…………

不論…………問題現在或將來如何發展，…………政府之立場，將不因之有所改變。外交部對大使館之抗議歉難接受。

使 舘 升 格
Elevation of Missions

例　　七

The Embassy of the ……… presents its compliments to the Diplomatic Missions accredited in ……… and has the honour to inform them that this Mission has been promoted to the rank of Embassy as from the………

The Embassy of the………avails itself of this opportunity to renew to the Diplomatic Missions accredited in……… the assurance of its highest consideration.

……………………………………

例　　八

L'Ambassade des ……… présente ses compliments aux Missions Diplomatiques accréditées en ……… et a l'honneur de porter à leur connaissance que par accord entre le Gouvernement ……… et le Gouvernement………, ils ont décidé d'élever au rang d'Ambassade leurs respectives Représentations à………et au………

La Légation des………est donc devenue Ambassade depuis le………

L'Ambassade des………saisit cette occasion pour renouveler aux Missions Diplomatiques accréditées en ………, les assurances de sa très haute considération.

……………………………………

AUX MISSIONS DIPLOMATIQUES
ACCREDITEES EN………

……………………………………

外 交 團 應 酬
Social Activities of Diplomatic Body

例　　九

The Chargé d'Affaires *ad interim* of .... presents his compliments to His Excellency the ·············· Ambassador, Dean of the Diplomatic Corps, and has the honor to acknowledge the receipt of His Excellency's note of ··············, ·············· regarding the farewell luncheon to be given on Thursday, March 24, at 1:30 p.m. in honor of His Excellency the Ambassador of the············Republic and Mrs. ·············, and His Excellency ············, Ambassador of·············.

The Chargé d'Affaires *ad interim* of ············ will be pleased to participate in the luncheon which he will attend with Mrs.·············. The Ambassador of the ············ will participate in the presentation of the two gifts.

The Chargé d'Affaires *ad interim* of ············ avails himself of this occasion to renew to the ············ Ambassador, Dean of the Diplomatic Corps, the assurances of his highest consideration.

例　　十

My dear Mr. Ambassador:

I wish to inform you that the 12th Anniversary Celebration of the Landing of the American Forces of Liberation at Leyte, will be held in Tacloban City on············under the auspices of the Tacloban City Lions' Club.

The Club has requested me to extend to you its invitation to be one of the Guests of Honor, together with the other accredited Ambassadors to ············, in the morning program and in the public popular luncheon where the American Ambassador has been invited to be the principal guest speaker. The Club will have the President of ··········· as its Principal Guest Speaker in the afternoon program. The President will arrive in Tacloban City at 3:00 o'clock in the afternoon of October 20.

A souvenir program will soon be prepared by the Club for the celebration. I would appreciate it if you could inform me as soon as possible whether you accept the invitation. Should the invitation be acceptable, I would further appreciate it if you could inform me whether you could be in Tacloban City in the morning of October 20.

With my highest esteem and regards, I am

Sincerely yours,
······························
Secretary

His Excellency
······················
Chinese Ambassador,
······················

例 十 一

The Secretary of Foreign Affairs presents his compliments to Their Excellencies and Messieurs the Chiefs of Mission and has the honor to transmit to the Chiefs of Mission the invitation of the Tenth World Jamboree Committee to a meeting-dinner of the 10th World Jamboree Board at 8:00 o'clock in the evening of ············, at the Winter Garden,···········Hotel.

President··········· will be the Guest of Honor and Speaker at this meeting.

It would be appreciated if the Chiefs of Mission could inform their acceptance of this invitation to the Protocol Division of the Department of Foreign Affairs.
·····································

例 十 二
NOTE CIRCULAIRE

Le Ministère Royal des Affaires Etrangères présente ses compliments aux Missions Diplomatiques accréditées à··········· et a l'honneur de porter à leur connaissance que Mercredi prochain 29 juin, un Te Deum sera chanté à la Cathédrale à 10 hrs. 30 en présence de L.L.M.M. le Roi et la Reine et des Membres de la Famille Royale.

Des places seront réservées à la Cathedrale pour MM. les Chefs des Missions, le personnel diplomatique des Missions, ainsi que pour leurs épouses.

Etant donné que les dispositions nécessaires afférant à la réservation des places assises pour MM. les Chefs des Missions et leurs épouses doivent être prises à temps, MM. les Chefs des Missions sont priés de bien vouloir faire connaître à la Direction du Protocole de ce Département Royal s'ils assisteront au Te Deum et s'ils seront accompagnés de leurs épouses.

Ce Département Royal saisit cette occasion pour renouveler aux Missions Diplomatiques accréditées à···········les assurances de sa très haute considération.-

....

Tenue: Uniforme ou habit et décorations

例 十 三

Le Grand Maréchalat de la Cour présente ses compliments à Son Excellence Monsieur le Doyen du Corps Diplomatique, Ambassadeur de ···········, et a l'honneur de lui faire savoir que Leurs Majestés le Roi et la Reine, se rendant officiellement en⋯⋯⋯, s'embarqueront à bord du Croiseur Helli Samedi prochain, le 7 Juin à 18.00 heures.

Son Excellence Monsieur le Doyen du Corps Diplomatique et Madame⋯⋯⋯sont invités de bien vouloir être présents au ⋯⋯⋯à 17.45 heures afin de saluer Leurs Majestés au départ.

Le Grand Maréchalat de la Cour saisit cette occasion pour exprimer à Son Excellence Monsieur le Doyen du Corps Diplomatique, Ambassadeur de ⋯⋯⋯, les assurances de sa plus haute considération.

Palais Royal d'⋯⋯⋯, le⋯⋯⋯

Tenue: Messieurs: Jacquette
       Dames: Toilette de Ville.

復　　文

L'Ambassade de⋯⋯⋯présente ses compliments au Grand Maréchalat de la Cour et a l'honneur d'accuser réception de sa Note du 2 Juin par laquelle celui-ci a bien voulu porter à sa connaissance que Leurs Majestés le Roi et la Reine, se Rendant officiellement en ⋯⋯⋯, s'embarqueront à bord du Croiseur Helli Samedi prochain, le 7 Juin à 18.00 heures.

L'Ambassadeur de ⋯⋯⋯ et Madame ⋯⋯⋯ ne manqueront pas d'être présents au ⋯⋯⋯ à 17.45 heures afin de saluer Leurs Majestés au départ.

L'Ambassadeur de ⋯⋯⋯ saisit cette occasion pour renouveler au Grand Maréchalat de la Cour les assurances de sa très haute considération.

⋯⋯⋯⋯⋯⋯⋯⋯⋯⋯⋯

Grand Maréchalat de la Cour
EN VILLE

例 十 四

Le Grand Maréchal de la Cour, Grand Maîre des Cérémonies, a l'honneur de porter à la connaissance de l'Ambassade de ·········· qu'à l'occasion de la Fête Nationale de Sa Majesté le Roi, Leurs Majestés le Roi et la Reine recevront au Palais Royal les félicitations de Messieurs les Chefs des Mission Diplomatiques ainsi que de leurs épouses, le Mercredi···········, à 11.40 heures.

Le Grand Maréchal de la Cour, Grand Maître des Cérémonies saisit cette occasion pour réitérer à l'Ambassade de ···········les assurances de sa très haute considération.

Palais Royal d'···········. le···········

(SEAL)

Arrivée au Palais Royal: 11.30 heures

Tenue: Messieurs: Uniforme, décorations.

Habit, gelet blanc, décorations

Dames: Toilette de Ville, chapeau, gants.

例 十 五

L'Ambassadeur de···········, Doyen du Corps Diplomatique, présente ses meilleurs compliments à Messieurs les Chefs de Mission accrédités à ··········· et a l'honneur de porter à leur connaissance qu'll a été proposé qu'à l'occasion du départ de ···········de LL.EE. l'Ambassadeur de Suisse et Madame···········, un diner leur soit offert de la part des Chefs de Mission. Ce diner aura lieu le Mardi 15 Décembre à 9 heures du soir au Pavillon de ··········· Tenue: Cravate noire. Les épouses des Chefs de Mission y assisteront également.

L'Ambassadeur de···········, Doyen du Corps Diplomatique,

prie Messieurs les Chefs de Mission de bien vouloir lui faire connaitre en temps utile s'ils participeront ainsi que leurs épouses au susdit diner et au cadeau traditionnel qui sera offert à leur Collègue en lui faisant parvenir, dans l'affirmative, un spécimen de leur signature destinée à être gravée sur celui–ci.

L'Ambassadeur de ·············, Doyen du Corps Diplomatique, saisit cette occasion pour renouveler à Messieurs les Chefs de Mission accrédités à ············ les assurances de sa très haute considération.

····································

例　十　六

L'Ambassade de ············ présente ses compliments au Ministère des Affaires Etrangères et a l'honneur de porter à Sa connaissance que le Gouvernement de la République de······ a decidé, par décret présidentiel, de décerner à Monsieur·········, ancien Chargé d'Affaires de············ en ············, la décoration de l'Ordre de l'Etoile Brillant, pour les services qu'il a rendus à la cause de l'amitié entre············et············

L'Ambassade de·······prie l'honorable Ministère de vouloir bien remettre au récipiendaire, avec ses meilleures félicitations, la décoration en question qu'elle s'empresse de Lui adresser sous pli séparé.

Le Diplome accompagnant la décoration n'étant pas encore arrivé, l'Ambassade de ············ se propose de le communiquer à l'honorable Ministère, aussitot qu'il Lui sera parvenu.

L'Ambassade de·······saisit cette occasion pour renouveler au Ministère des Affaires Etrangères, les assurances de sa très haute considération.

例　十　七

L'Ambassade de⋯⋯⋯présente ses compliments à l'Ambas— sade de ⋯⋯⋯⋯ et a l'honneur de Lui parvenir ci‑joint, le montant de ⋯⋯⋯⋯, en participation de cette Ambassade à l'achat du cadeau pour Mademoiselle⋯⋯⋯⋯

L'Ambassade de⋯⋯⋯⋯, en remerciant l'Ambassade de⋯ ⋯⋯⋯⋯, saisit cette occasion pour Lui renouveler les assurances de sa très haute considération.

⋯⋯⋯⋯⋯⋯, le ⋯⋯⋯⋯⋯⋯

例　十　八

L'Ambassade de ⋯⋯⋯⋯ présente ses compliments aux Missions Diplomatiques accréditées à⋯⋯⋯⋯⋯et a l'honneur de Les informer qu'à l'occasion du mariage de Mademoiselle ⋯⋯⋯ ⋯⋯⋯, le ⋯⋯⋯⋯⋯ et, sur la proposition faite par Messieurs les Chefs de Missions, un cadeau collectif consistant en un service en argent massif composé de quatre pièces et d'un plateau sur lequel a été gravée l'inscription:

"LE CORPS DIPLOMATIQUE ACCREDITE A⋯⋯⋯⋯

Le 24, Mars⋯⋯⋯⋯⋯"

a été présenté le⋯⋯⋯⋯à Mademoiselle⋯⋯⋯⋯⋯Le cadeau était accompagné d'une carte exprimant à la jeune mariée les félicitations et les voeux du Corps Diplomatique.

Le prix du service (y compris le travail de gravure) étant de⋯⋯⋯⋯⋯, la cotisation individuelle de chacune des 41 missions résidant à ⋯⋯⋯⋯⋯, s'élève à ⋯⋯⋯⋯⋯ Ces cotisations peuvent être adressées à l'Ambassade de⋯⋯⋯⋯⋯où l'on peut consulter les factures se rapportant à cet achat.

L'Ambassade de········saisit cette occasion pour renouveler aux Missions Diplomatiques, les assurances de sa très haute considération.

············, le ··················,·····

Aux Missions Diplomatiques
accréditées à···········

例　十　九

Le Directeur Général du Protocole présente ses compliments à Messieurs les Chefs de Mission et a l'honneur de les informer que l'ouverture de la Grande Assemblée Nationale de············ aura lieu le Mercredi 1er Novembre à 15 heures.

············' le ··················

Aux Missions Diplomatiques　　　　　　　　Tenue: Jaquette
··················,·······

簽證與出入境
Visa: Exit and Entry

例　二　十

The Embassy of the Republic of············presents its compliments to the Department of Foreign Affairs of the······ ······and has the honor to request that the attached diplomatic passport of Mrs.··········, wife of the··········· Ambassador, be appropriately visaed for re-entry into ··············

Enclosure: Diplomatic Passport No.············

例 二 十 一

The Embassy of the Republic of .... presents its compliments to the Department of Foreign Affairs of .... and has the honor to inform the Department that, as in the previous years, the ············ Government is sending two naval vessels,············and············, to········for ferrying the Overseas ············Students' Goodwill Mission from············to···········The Mission comprises about ············ students. The said naval vessels are expected to arrive at········on or about···········and will dock in ths harbor for three days prior to their departure.

The Embassy will greatly appreciate it if the Department will be so good as to request the authorities concerned to grant clearance and facilities to the aforesaid vessels and their officers and enlisted men upon their arrival and departure.

例 二 十 二

The Ambassador of the Republic of ············ presents his compliments to the Secretary of Foreign Affairs of···········and has the honor to inform the Secretary that the Government information office of the Republic of···········sent one (1) case of books to the Press Counsellor's Office of the Embassy from ···········by S.S.···········which arrived in···········on···········

The Ambassador would much appreciate it if the Secretary would be good enough to notify the authorities concerned to exempt the aforesaid shipment from taxation and facilitate its release.

Enclosed herewith please find the bill of lading of said shipment.

Encl:a/s

例 二 十 三

The Department of Foreign Affairs presents its compliments to the Embassy of the Republic of·········and has the honor to request that ·········· Passport No. ··········, which was issued by the Department on··········, to Mr.··········, be not honored should said person apply for a visa in that Mission.

The Department would likewise appreciate it if it could be advised of any attempt said person would make to travel to the territories within the jurisdiction of the Mission.

The Department avails itself of this opportunity to renew the assurances of its highest consideration.

例 二 十 四

L'Ambassade de·········présente ses compliments empressés au Département du Protocole et a l'honneur de Le Prier de vouloir bien accorder un visa de sortie ainsi qu'un laissez–passer à Monsieur l'Ambassadeur de ·········· et Madame ·········· qui quitteront prochainement··········pour se rendre à l'étranger.

Avec ses meilleurs remerciements anticipés, l'Ambassade de··········saisit cette occasion pour renouveler à l'honorable Département du Protocole, les assurances de sa très haute considération.

例 二 十 五

L'Ambassade de ⋯⋯⋯ présente ses compliments au Ministère des Affaires Etrangères et a l'honneur de le prier de bien vouloir accorder un visa de sortie aller et retour pour l'étranger valable pour trois mois et pour plusieurs voyages à Son Excellence⋯⋯⋯, Ambassadeur de⋯⋯⋯, qui se rend en Suisse et en Autriche accompagné de sa femme.

L'Ambassade de⋯⋯⋯ saisit cette occasion pour renouveler au Ministère des Affaires Etrangères les assurances de sa très haute considération.

例 二 十 六

La Légation de ⋯⋯⋯ présente ses compliments les plus empressés au Ministère des Affaires Etrangères et a l'honneur de le prier, avec ses remerciements anticipés, de vouloir bien accorder son visa diplomatique et délivrer un laisser–passer en faveur de Monsieur⋯⋯⋯, Chargé d'Affaires, qui se rend à l'Etranger.

例 二 十 七

L'Ambassade de⋯⋯⋯présente ses compliments empressés à la Légation Royale d'Egypte, et a l'honneur de La prier de vouloir bien accorder aussi rapidement que possible, un visa de transit ainsi qu'un laissez–passer à M. le Capitaine⋯⋯⋯, Attaché Militaire Adjoint près cette Ambassade, qui se rend en⋯⋯⋯via l'Egypte.

Avec ses meilleurs remerciements anticipés, l'Ambassade de⋯⋯⋯saisit cette occasion pour renouveler à l'honorable Légation Royale, les assurances de sa haute considération.

例 二 十 八

L'Ambassade de France Présente ses compliments à l'Ambassade de la République de Chine et a le plaisir de lui faire connaitre que tous les ressortissants de la Republique Chinoise, domiciliés aux Philippines et en possession d'un passeport en cours de validité délivré par leur gouvernement, peuvent désormais obtenir directement de cette Ambassade un visa d'entrée en France valable trois mois.

L'autorisation de Département ne demeure nécessaire que pour les visas au–dessus de trois mois ou pour les non-domicilliés sur le territoire des Philippines.

L'Ambassade de France saisit cette occasion pour renouveler à l'Ambassade de la Republique de Chine les assurances de sa haute considération./.

例 二 十 九

En réponse à la Note No.············du 14 novembre courant de l'honorable Ministère des Affairs Etrangères, ayant trait à la décision du Gouvernement············d'exempter de l'autorisation préalable l'octroi des visas d'entrée aux membres des Missions Diplomatiques et Consulaires de carrière en············, munis de passeports diplomatiques, ainsi que pour les visas de transit des diplomates étrangers, compris dans les catégories susmentionnées, qui traversent la············, l'Ambassade de············a l'honneur de l'informer que la············ayant admis le principe de réciprocité, appliquera la même procédure à partir du············

L'Ambassade de············saisit cette occasion pour renouveler à l'honorable Ministère, les assurances de sa très haute considération.

例 三 十

L'Ambassáde de Chine présente ses compliments empressés à l'Ambassade de France, et a l'honneur de La prier de
vouloir bien accorder un visa à Mr.············, ressortissant
Chinois, désireux de se rendre en France pour y voir un ami
nommé············

Avec ses remerciements anticipés, l'Ambassade de Chine
saisit cette occasion pour renouveler à l'honorable Ambassade
de France, les assurances de sa très haute considération.

雜　件
Miscellaneous

例 三 十 一
羅斯福總統謝伊朗國王招待及贈禮

Tehran, December 1, 1943.

Your Majesty,

I was very much pleased to see you yesterday when you
welcomed me to your country in the name of the Iranian
people. Your gesture is one that emphasizes again the more
than friendly feeling that has always existed between our two
nations. I was delighted to have had this chance to make
Your Majesty's acquaintance.

I have received the magnificent carpet, the gracious gift
of Your Majesty. This carpet will serve to remind both myself
and the American people of the generous hospitality of the
Iranian nation. I am truly grateful.

Your Majesty's invitation to be a guest at your palace as
well as your offer to meet me at the airport upon my arrival
and to provide a guard of honor have been conveyed to me

and I am most appreciative. Much to my regret, the circumstances of my visit, as you are no doubt aware, have made it impossible for me to avail myself of these kind offers, much as I would have liked to have done so.

I cannot emphasize too strongly how much I have been touched by all of these truly friendly gestures on the part of Your Majesty. I shall leave Iran with regret at not having had an opportunity to extend my acquaintance with you and to have seen more of your country and your people. The American people have for many years been cognizant of the friendly sentiments of the Iranian people, and the hospitality shown by Your Majesty in their name will serve to keep this realization alive for many years to come.

Iran has always occupied a warm spot in American hearts, more than ever now that we are brothers in arms. We know the part Iran is playing in the common struggle and our hope is that when peace at last comes, the spirit of working together that now exists between our two peoples will continue unchecked in peaceful labors.

I take this opportunity to thank Your Majesty again for all the gestures of friendliness and hospitality you have shown me and to wish Your Majesty the greatest happiness both for yourself and for the people of your ancient land.

With my sincere regards, I am,

Faithfully yours,

(Signed) Franklin D. Roosevelt

I greatly hope that we shall have the pleasure of a visit from you to Washington.

伊朗國王復羅斯福總統函

Tehran, December 6, 1943.

Dear Mr. President,

Your Minister duly delivered the framed photograph which Your Excellency was good enough to present to me, just before your departure, as a souvenir of your memorable visit to Tehran.

This handsome gift, a very good likeness, stands in a prominent place in my study and will always remind me of your great personality and the interesting conversation we had together on November 30th.

Your Excellency's kind letter of December 1st has also been gratefully received. The cordial sentiments therein expressed are entirely reciprocated, and I look forward to an ever–increasing cooperation between our two countries in the arts of peace to our mutual advantage.

Let me assure Your Excellency that the friendship of the American people is very precious to us; my constant desire will be to foster closer ties between Iran and the United States of America which have already been brought so near to one another in the common struggle for freedom,

It is indeed a matter for gratification that the momentous Tehran Conference was a success. We have to be particularly grateful to Your Excellency for your share in obtaining approval of the satisfactory Communiqué issued yesterday regarding Iran, in the drafting of which Mr. ··········, Your able and distinguished representative, has taken an outstanding part.

The kind invitation to visit Washington, extended by Your Excellency, is much appreciated and I hope to be able to avail myself of it and to have the pleasure of seeing You again as soon as circumstances permit.

With the assurance of my friendship and highest consideration, I remain, dear Mr. President,

Yours sincerely,

(Signed) Mohammad Reza Pahlavi

例 三 十 二

The Cairo Communiqué
December 1, 1943.

President Roosevelt, Generalissimo Chiang Kai-shek and Prime Minister Churchill, together with their respective military and diplomatic advisers, have completed a conference in North Africa. The following general statement was issued:

"The several military missions have agreed upon future military operations against Japan. The three great Allies expressed their ressolve to bring unrelenting pressure against their brutal enemies by sea, land and air. This pressure is already rising.

"The three great Allies are fighting this war to restrain and punish the aggression of Japan. They covet no gain for themselves and have no thought of territorial expansion. It is their purpose that Japan shall be stripped of all the islands in the Pacific which she has sezied or occupied since the beginning of the first World War in 1914, and that all the territories Japan has stolen from the Chinese, such as Manchuria, Formosa, and the Pescadores, shall be restored to the Republic of China. Japan will also be expelled from all other territories which she has taken by violence and greed. The aforesaid three great powers, mindful of the enslavement of the people of Korea, are determined that in due course Korea shall become free and independent.

"With these objects in view the three Allies, in harmony with those of the United Nations at war with Japan, will continue to persevere in the serious and prolonged operations necessary to procure the unconditional surrender of Japan."

例 三 十 三

Cairo, December 6, 1943

My dear King Farouk,

It is a cause of profound regret to me that owing to Your Majesty's absence from Cairo following your regrettable accident I am forced to leave Egypt without having the pleasure of meeting you.

My visit to your country has been brief, and the exigencies of my duties while here prevented me from enjoying all that Egypt holds of interest and beauty. I wish, however, to assure you that I have been happy to be here and that I appreciate deeply the hospitality of this land and the signal courtesies which you have proffered.

I hope that I may visit Egypt again and that then circumstances will permit our meeting. In the meanwhile I extend to you my best wishes for your speedy recovery and for the welfare and happiness of your people.

Again with many thanks, I am,

Your sincere friend,

(Signed) F.D.R.

例 三 十 四

宋子文代表中國政府商請美政府派遣軍事顧問團赴華

Washington, August 7, 1941.

Dear Mr. President:

I have been directed by Generalissimo Chiang Kai-shek respectfully to request you and your Secretary of War to send a military mission to China in the immediate future. Such a mission would immensely increase the value of the Lend-Lease assistance you are supplying to China and which, we understand, is at the point where it is about to reach considerable volume. The Generalissimo points out that the importance of such a mission at this time is particularly emphasized by events in China. China has just formally broken off diplomatic relations with the German Government. The memory of the assistance given our army in the first stages of its resistance to Japan by the military mission of the German army is still significant in the minds of our army. At this time of the severance of relations with Germany, it would be most symbolic to have the memory of this German army assistance replaced by the presence of a mission from the American army coincident with the arrival of American materials.

Yours respectfully,

(Signed) TSE VUN SOONG

羅斯福總統答覆宋氏決派軍事顧問團赴華

Washington, August 20, 1941.

Dear Dr. Soong:

I am happy to comply with the request of Generalissimo Chiang Kai-shek, conveyed to me through your letter of August 7, that an American mission be sent to China. The Secretary of War has selected as chief of the mission Brigadier General Magruder, who is now assembling his mission and will depart, as soon as possible, for Chungking.

I trust that this mission will aid China in her valiant struggle.

Sincerely yours,

(Signed) Franklin D. Roosevelt

例 三 十 五

Excellency:

I have the honor, in accordance with instructions from the Department of State, to transmit herewith for Your Excellency's information one copy each of Department of State press releases concerning the adherence of ………… and the Commonwealth of the ………… to the Declaration by United Nations.

Accept, Excellency, the renewed assurances of my highest consideration.

(signed) American Ambassador

Enclosures:

Press releases, as
Stated above.

Excellency:

In reference to previous exchanges of views on different occasions between the Department of Foreign Affairs and the ··········Embassy in ··········regarding the proposed conclusion of a cultural agreement between the Government of the Republic of ··········· and the Government of the Republic of ···········, I have the honor to enclose herewith a copy of the revised text of the draft convention or agreement which has been agreed to by my Government, together with a copy of the··········text of the agreement.

It will be noted that in the attached draft, a ratification clause has been inserted in the agreement in accordance with the expressed desire of the Department.

Should Your Excellency's Government agree to the text of the draft attached herewith, I am pleased to inform Your Excellency that my Government is prepared to have it signed at any time to be arranged.

Accept, Excellency, the renewed assurances of my highest consideration.

例 三 十 七

Excellency:

I have the honor to inform Your Excellency that the Bureau of Education of the Taiwan Provincial Government, Republic of China, is desirous of inviting Dr. ··········· of the ··········Government to proceed to Taipei to act as an ádviser on the Community School Project initiated by the said Provincial Government. It would be much appreciated if Your Excellency would be so kind as to transmit this invitation to the pertinent authorities of the⋯⋯⋯Government and to facilitate the early acceptance and departure of Dr. ⋯⋯⋯⋯

Accept, Excellency, the renewed assurances of my highest consideration.

(Chinese Ambassador)

例 三 十 八

The ⋯⋯⋯⋯ Embassy presents its compliments to the Ministry of Foreign Affairs and has the honor to state that instructions have been received from the Secretary of State to approach the Ministry with a view to obtaining the consent of the ⋯⋯⋯⋯⋯ Government to the publication of certain documents in Foreign Relations of the United States ⋯⋯⋯⋯

In this connection the Embassy has the honor to transmit herewith uncorrected proofs of the following documents.

1. ⋯⋯⋯⋯⋯⋯⋯⋯⋯⋯⋯⋯⋯⋯⋯⋯⋯⋯⋯⋯⋯⋯⋯⋯⋯⋯⋯⋯⋯⋯⋯⋯⋯⋯⋯⋯⋯
⋯⋯⋯⋯⋯⋯⋯⋯⋯⋯⋯⋯⋯⋯⋯⋯⋯⋯⋯⋯⋯⋯⋯⋯⋯⋯

2. ⋯⋯⋯⋯⋯⋯⋯⋯⋯⋯⋯⋯⋯⋯⋯⋯⋯⋯⋯⋯⋯

It may be observed that inasmuch as the proof will be carefully compared with the documents on file in the Department of State, it will not be necessary for the Ministry to scrutinize the proof for accuracy of text.

The Embassy has the honor to request the favor of an early reply.

Enclosures: Proofs

例 三 十 九

依照國際法及慣例，領事官在原則上不能享受一般外交官享有之不出席當地民刑法庭作證的豁免權，但外交官兼領事官（如目前各國大使舘的領事部官員）或獨立領事舘的領事官，其本國外交代表或其本國政府認爲其領事官不便出庭作證時，可以拒絕爲之，亦可請法庭派員到使舘錄取證詞，這是折衷辦法。請參考例三十九及例四十。

The Embassy of the Republic of⋯⋯⋯⋯presents its compliments to the Department of Foreign Affairs of⋯⋯⋯⋯ and, with reference to the Department's notes, Nos⋯⋯⋯⋯and ⋯⋯⋯⋯, of August 12 and September 2, ⋯⋯⋯⋯respectiviey, requesting the Embassy's assistance in having a subpoena served on the Secretary of the Embassy to appear at the Court of First Instance of⋯⋯⋯⋯ on ⋯⋯⋯⋯, has the honor to state that, much as it likes to render assistance to the afore-mentioned court in regard to the hearing of Criminal Case No.⋯⋯⋯⋯(People of⋯⋯⋯⋯versus⋯⋯⋯⋯), the Embassy regrets that it is not prepared in this case to waive the exemption normally granted to the members of an Embassy and/or professional consuls to be subpoenaed as witnesses, an exemption which is generally recognized as a basic principle of international law and practice. The subpeonas attached are therefore returned herewith.

Encls: as stated

The Embassy of the Republic of .... presents its compliments to the Department of Foreign Affairs of .... and has the honor to refer to a subpeona sent by the Court of First Instance of the City of··········dated···········,requesting the presence and testimony of the official–in–charge of the Embassy at the hearing of Case No··········(People of the ···········vs.············, et al).

The Embassy wishes to inform the Department that in this case the Government of the Republic of··········is waiving the immunity of the official–in–charge of the Embassy and has authorized him to give such testimony in written form to the court officials of the Government of··········at the premise of the Embassy of the Republic of···········in···········

The Embassy of the Republic of··············presents its compliments to the Department of Foreign Affairs and has the honor to request for three (3) copies each of Vol. 1, No. 2 and Vol. III, No. 1 of the Department of Foreign Affairs Review for transmittal to the Ministry of Foreign Affairs in ············

It is further requested that the Department be good enough to continue to send to this Embassy three copies each of the succeeding issues of the Review.

Should there be any charge for copies in addition to those which the Department is prepared to distribute to the foreign missions, the Embassy will be glad to shoulder the expenses.

The Embassy would be most grateful if the Department would make necessary arrangements on this matter.

例 四 十 二

The Embassy of the Republic of⋯⋯⋯⋯⋯presents its compliments to the Department of Foreign Affairs of⋯⋯⋯⋯ and has the honor to send along herewith a set of "Compilation of the Laws of the Republic of China" in 3 volumes published by the Legislative Yuan (Parliament).

The Embassy would deeply appreciate it if the Department would be so good as to forward the volumes to the Library of the Congress of⋯⋯⋯⋯as a gift from the Chinese Legislative Yuan to its counterpart in the⋯⋯⋯⋯⋯

例 四 十 三

The Embassy of the Republic of⋯⋯⋯⋯⋯presents its compliments to the Department of Foreign Affairs of⋯⋯⋯⋯ and has the honor to request for two (2) copies of the latest statistical report on export and import of the Bureau of Customs. The aforementioned report will be used as reference for the purpose of economic research of the concerned authorities in⋯⋯⋯⋯

The Embassy would appreciate it very much if the Department would be good enough to contact the Bureau of Customs on this matter. Should there be any charge for the copies of the report, the Embassy will be glad to shoulder the expense.

例 四 十 四

Dear Mr. Secretary:

I wish to thank you for your letter of ...., together with a copy of the Report of the Board of National Education for the years 1955–1957.

The Report is most informative and has given me a better understanding and appreciation of the general edutional policies of ....I am grateful for your thoughtfulness in making it available to me.

With warm personal regards,

Sincerely yours,

....

例 四 十 五

Dear Mr. Secretary:

I wish to thank you for your thoughtfulness in sending me a copy of the picture taken during your call at my office the other day.

I shall treasure it as a momento of the cordial relations between our countries as well as our personal friendship.

My assistants join me in sending you and your staff our best wishes for your continued success.

Sincerely yours,

....

例 四 十 六

The Embassy of the Republic of·············presents its compliments to the Department of Foreign Affairs and has the honor to acknowledge the receipt of the Department's memorandum No.·············, dated ············, ············, regarding the First ············International Film Festival. Pursuant to the Department's request, the Embassy is appending hereto a brief description of·············film entries at the Festival and will transmit the still pictures required by the Festival Committee as soon as they are received by the Embassy. The Embassy has also conveyed to the ············Government, as well as film organizations in············, the Committee's invitation to send a delegation to the Festival.

例 四 十 七

The Embassy of the Republic of·············presents its compliments to the Department of Foreign Affairs of············ and has the honor to request for the assistance of the latter in obtaining a complete list of the nationwide youth organizations in ············. The materials in question will be used for the purpose of promoting friendly ties and better understanding between the youth organizations of our two countries.

The Embassy wishes particularly to secure the following details of information on the············youth organizations: (1) organization, (2) activities and history; and (3) responsible persons and addresses.

The Embassy will appreciate it very much if the Department will be so good as to extend the necessary assistance on this matter.

The Embassy of the Republic of·············presents its compliments to the Royal Ministry of Foreign Affairs and referring to the Embassy's Note No. ···········, dated ············ and the Royal Ministry's Note No. ············, dated ············, concerning the collision of the ··········· cargo ship "············" with the ··········· fishing boat " ············ ", has the honor to request, through the Royal Ministry, compensation by the appropriate···········authorities in favor of the said fishing boat on the strength of proofs submitted by the owner of the said fishing boat, together with two copies of pictures of the damaged boat.

According to the report of the owner of the fishing boat to the ··········· Government, the damage done to the boat by the···········cargo ship "············" cost US$···········The loss of cordage, lamps and the fishes already caught and then freed after the ship was damaged amounted to US$···········The total loss and damage thus came to US$ ············ The report has been certified by the···········Government as correct.

The Embassy wishes to attach the two copies of the pictures mentioned above to the Ministry for the reference of the appropriate···········authorities and hopes to hear from the Ministry as soon as possible.

The Embassy avails itself of this opportunity to extend to the Royal Ministry the assurances of its highest consideration.

Encl.: As Stated.
·····················

例 四 十 九

MEMORANDUM

His Britannic Majesty's Embassy present their compliments
to the⋯⋯⋯⋯Ministry of Foreign Affairs and have the honour
to refer to the Stabilisation Fund Agreement recently concluded between representatives of the⋯⋯⋯⋯Ministry of Finance
and His Majesty's Treasury which provides *inter alia* that "at
least one member of the Board shall be appointed by the⋯⋯⋯
⋯⋯Government at the request of and on the recommendation
of the Treasury."

His Majesty's Embassy have now been instructed to inform
the⋯⋯⋯⋯Government that the Chancellor of the Exchequer
recommends, as a temporary measure, Mr. ⋯⋯⋯⋯ and requests
that the⋯⋯⋯⋯Government will appoint him to be a temporary member of the Stabilisation Board in accordance with the
above mentioned provision.

例 五 十

Monsieur le Ministre,

Sur les instructions de mon Gouvernement, j'ai l'honneur
de porter a la connaissance de Votre Excellence que par décret
du Yuan Exécutif en date du 12 Janvier 1946, le Gouvernement
de Chine déclare que, à la suite du retour de Taiwan (Formose)
à la Chine, les habitants de ce territoire ayant perdu leur
nationalité Chinoise par suite de l'agression ennemie, sont
réintégrés dans leur nationalité Chinoise à la date du 25 Octobre
1945.

Veuillez agréer, Monsieur le Ministre, les assurances de
ma plus haute considération.

(Chinese Ambassador)

例 五 十 一

L'Ambassade de ············· présente ses compliments au Ministère Royal des Affaires Etrangères et a l'honneur de Lui faire parvenir, sous pli séparé, pour Sa documentation, un exemplaire du Recueil des Traités conclus entre la République de Chine et les Etats étrangers pour les années 1927–1957.

L'Ambassade de ········saisit cette occasion pour renouveler au Ministère Royal des Affaires Etrangères les assurances de sa très haute considération.

例 五 十 二

En réponse à la Note-Verbale de la Lègation de ············, datée du ··········· Sub No, ············, le Ministère des Affaires Etrangères a l'honneur de Lui faire parvenir ci–jointe une liste contenant les numéros des Lois et réglements ainsi que ceux des Articles de ces Lois et règlements, concernant les droits et obligations des commerçants étrangers établis en ············. Annexe: 1.

例 五 十 三

Le Ministère des Affaires Etrangères a l'honneur de communiquer aux Missions Diplomatiques accréditées à·········· que tout avion étranger qui viendrait survoler le territoire et les eaux territoriales··········sans avoir obtenu au préalable l'autorisation prescrite par la réglementation concernant la navigation aérienne en············, s'expose à un danger certain du fait qu'il aura à essuyer le feu des forces armées du pays.

Ce Ministère prie les Missions Diplomatiques de vouloir bien, dans l'intérêt de la sécurité de la navigation aérienne

attirer l'attenion des autorités intéressées de leur pays sur ce
qui précède.

....

例 五 十 四

NOTE CIRCULAIRE

Le Ministère Royal des Affaires Etrangères présente ses
compliments aux Missions Diplomatiques accréditées en···········
et a l'honneur de porter à leur connaissance qu'il lui est
revenue que certaines Missions se sont adressées de nouveau
directement aux Ministères et Services compétents sans l'en-
tremise de ce Ministère.

Cette pratique étant contraire à l'usage en vigueur en······
······, ce Département a l'honneur de rappeler aux Missions
Diplomatiques sa Note Circulaire No.··············· du ···········et
de les prier de bien vouloir s'y conformer.

Ce Ministère Royal saisit cette occasion pour réitérer aux
Missions Diplomatiques accréditées en ··········· les assurances
de sa très haute considération.

....

例 五 十 五

Monsieur le Grand Maréchal,

J'ai l'honneur de remettre sous ce pli à Votre Excellence
un télégramme adressé par le Maréchal ···········, Président de
la République de···········, à Sa Majesté le Roi en vous priant
de bien vouloir avoir l'amabilité de le remettre à Sa Majesté.

Je saisis cette occassion, Monsieur le Grand Maréchal,
pour renouveler à Votre Excellence les assurances de ma très
haute considération.

Annexe: a télégramme

例 五 十 六
NOTE CIRCULAIRE

Le Ministère Royal des Affaires Etrangères prèsente ses compliments aux Missions Diplomatiques accréditées à⋯⋯⋯⋯ et a l'honneur de lui faire parvenlr ci-inclus un spécimen de notice biographique avec prière d'ajouter une notice similaire aux communications ayant trait à l'affection auprés de ces Missions de nouveaux Attachés Militaires, Navals et de l'Air ainsi que de leurs Assistants.

Ce Département Royal saisit cette occasion pour renouveler aux Missions Diplomatiques accréditées à⋯⋯⋯⋯les assurances de sa très haute considération.

⋯⋯⋯⋯⋯⋯⋯⋯⋯⋯⋯⋯

例 五 十 七

Mon Cher Ambassadeur,

Je viens de recevoir avec beaucoup de plaisir les deux très belles potiches⋯⋯⋯⋯que vous avez bien voulu me faire remettre. Je vous en remercie sincèrement.

Vous connaissez ma passion pour les objets d'art ⋯⋯⋯⋯. La vue de ces potiches que J'ai placées à une place de choix, sera pour nous un plaisir toujours renouvelé.

Je vous prie, mon Cher Ambassadeur, d'agréer avec mes meilleurs voeux de bonne année pour vous et l'Ambassadrice, l'assurance de mes sentiments les plus cordiaux.

(Signed)⋯⋯⋯⋯⋯⋯⋯

附　　錄

APPENDIX

一、外交名詞選編

Glossary of Diplomatic Terms

Accession

國際條約簽定後，凡未參加簽字者得於事後加入，法文稱爲 adhésion。此項事後加入必須在條約本身上有如此規定，或經創始會員國之邀請加入。

Acte Final

國際會議後每草擬一相當正式文件，記載會議中所通過之議案及會議大要。如會後簽訂條約，亦須加以說明，此項文書稱爲最後條款。

Additional Articles

附加條款係於國際間協定簽訂後有關次要問題而補簽之條款，或對正式條文加以解釋之條款。附加條款應與正約同時獲得批准。

Ad hoc

職此之故，爲此。For this particular purpose。

Ad interim

當時 In the meanwhile。

Ad referendum 與 Sub spe rati

當派遣國元首或接受國元首死亡,嚴格言之,其外交代表之任務應即終止，但在新國書未奉到前，該外交代表仍可繼續進行談判，盼所談各節能得到其本國元首之批准，是謂之 Sub spe rati。在今日交通發達之情況下，外交代表隨時可以請示其本國政府，如遇對方提供建議，外交代表最多可以視作參考，容再核議 ad referendum,不能因此約束其本人或其所代表之政府，意即俟得到其本國政府批准後可接受此項建議。

A fortiori

有較强之理由 With all the stronger reason, all the more.

Agreement

協定不僅兩國政府間可以簽訂，即一國政府與聯合國及其專門機關亦經常簽訂。顧名思義，凡協定皆雙方獲得同意之文書，簽訂後該文書即發生拘束力。聯合國與各國政府間多簽訂協定，而不簽訂條約或專約之原因，據說由於聯合國欲避免用條約或專約方式而要求對各國享有特權。

Agrément

一國派遣使節，事先必須得到未來駐在國政府之同意，習慣上為避免個人之受窘起見，一國政府多於事先秘密的以私人資格探詢對方國政府之意見，如反應良好，可正式向對方徵求同意，其方式或經由該國卸任的使節，或經由該國的臨時代辦，或向擬派往國家之使節接洽，請其向其本國政府探詢意見。或經由其他方式。對方國政府可以拒絕接受，而不必說明拒絕之理由，派遣國對此項拒絕多不追究其理由，亦不得視此為不友好之行為。因為一個獨立主權國家自有全權決定接受或不接受另一國家之使節，事實上派遣一個不受歡迎之使節前往他國駐紮，自無法盼其促進邦交，達成使命。

Aide-mémoire

備忘錄為外交文書中之一，無照會節略之有頭有尾，亦不需簽名。如大使奉本國政府訓令，約晤駐在國外交部長洽談公務時，洽談畢，大使多將事先準備之備忘錄留交外交部長。

Alternat

簽訂國際條約或某種重要文書時，凡與會國均可保有原約本一份。為使各國能同等享有首次簽約權之榮譽與地位，國際間多用輪替辦法，或首次簽約權（alternat）。即約本由甲國持有者，甲國元首及其全權代表列名在先，簽名亦在先。同樣約本由乙國持有者，乙國元首及其全權代表列名在先，其簽名亦在其他各國之前，如是每一國家皆有機會享有榮譽地位。

Ambassador-at-large

有譯爲"無任所大使"或"巡廻大使"者，亦有稱爲"不定大使"者，爲一非正式之駐外使節，無固定任所，有事政府即派遣之。美國最喜派此類大使，其職權有時且能超出於普通大使之上。

Ambassadors and Ministers

大使爲外交代表中之最高級外交官，在昔爲君主或國家元首之私人代表。公使乃國家之代表 (the representative of the state)。在君主時代，選派大使爲君主之代表，可以使其享受種種特權，今日各國實行民主立憲，大使公使皆代表國家及人民，亦同享各種外交特權，故今日兩者之區別，僅爲官階 (rank) 之大小與席位 (precedence) 之先後。

A priori

自因至果 From the cause to the effect.

Arbitration

仲裁法庭法官由爭執雙方自行選擇，糾紛案件移請仲裁時，雙方應有誠意接受判決。仲裁法庭之判決係根據法律作成，故有拘束力。

Asylum

政治犯逃往外國避難，照一般接受之慣例，該犯不能遣返其本國。在緊急情況下亦有逃入駐在本國首都之外國使館避難者。在拉丁美洲各國，因革命與政變不時發生，此種情事更屢見不鮮。

Attaché

一般譯爲隨員，爲大使館或公使館內最低級之外交官員，位於三等秘書之下，現在若干國家已將此類外交官名稱取消。大使館內有另設置一類軍官者，主要擔任軍事情報之搜集，分別稱爲海陸空軍武官 (Naval Attaché, Military Attaché, Air Attaché)，由國內軍政部門選派。另外若干國家之有關機關亦派遣 Press Attaché, Commercial Attaché 一類官員，附在駐外使館內，稱爲新聞專員，商務專員等。

Bona fide

誠實 In good faith.

Capitulations

在昔强大國家常利用條約强迫弱小國家，尤其 non-Christian 國家，給予强大國家國民以種種特權之優待，如免稅及不受當地政府法庭之審判，這類條約統稱爲 Capitulations,享受此類特權之國家稱爲 Capitulatory Powers.

Chancery (Chancellery)

大使館或公使館館長及館員之辦公處。

Chargé d'Affaires

大使或公使短期離職時，指派使館最高級館員暫行代理館務，稱臨時代辦 Chargé d'Affaires, ad interim. 亦有兩國因事暫不派遣使節駐紮，而派一正式代辦駐在對方國首都，在外交團其地位較臨時代辦略高。此種代辦係對駐在國外交部長派遣者，非對駐在國元首派遣。常駐或正式代辦法文稱 Chargé d'Affaires en titre, 或 Chargé d'Affaires ad hoc, 或 Chargé d'Affaires en pied 習慣上常駐代辦僅稱 Chargé d'Affaires.

Chargé des Affaires

當兩國之正式邦交無法維持時，使館之文卷及其他財產卽交由一低級職員看管，此項職員卽稱爲 chargé des affaires.

Compromis

若國家與國家間因事引起爭執,結果各方同意以仲裁方法解決之，英文稱爲 Special Agreement. 移送仲裁時應說明 (1) 糾紛之內容 (2) 組織仲裁法庭之方法 (3) 仲裁法庭設立地點等。

Conciliation

普通在聽取爭執雙方之意見後，爲調解起見，爭執案件乃移請一特設之委員會作成建議，設法調處,但此項建議本身並無拘束力。

Consular Commission or Letter of Provision

領事委任文憑或委任狀由國家元首簽署及外交部長副署頒發，說明派某某爲駐某地方領事，所有關係該地方本國人民種種以及商務利害，均歸該領事依法保護，請駐在國政府承認其領事地位，並允其執行領事職務，如駐在國承認接受，則須頒發領事證書或認可狀 Letter of Exequatur.

Consular Exequatur

爲駐在國認可外國所派領事而簽發之文書，稱爲"領事證書"或"領事許可證"，或"認可狀"。領事官有此項證書即可執行其職權。

Consular service

領事官專注意於商務及經濟問題，其主要職務在增進本國與駐在國間之通商利益，及保護本國僑胞並辦理護照簽證等事宜。關於領事之派遣與接受，往往依據兩國所簽訂之條約。

Convention

專約雖非絕對必需的，但常爲國際間多數國家簽訂而有創制法律效果之協定，其形式亦相當莊嚴。

Corps diplomatique

英文稱 Diplomatic body 或 Corps 外交團是派駐在同一政府各使館館長之集合 L'ensemble des chefs de mission accrédités auprè du même gouvernement forme le Corps diplomatique. 這僅由各國派駐之大公使組成之外交團乃狹義的。實則除大公使外應包括參事、秘書、隨員、陸海空軍武官、文化、新聞、經濟、商務參事、專員等及其夫人與成年女兒 The Diplomatic Body comprises all the heads of missions, counsellors, secretaries and attachés, both paid and honorary, including military, naval, air and commercial attachés, chaplains and all other members who are on the diplomatic establishment of their respective countries. At many capitals a list of the diplomatic body, compiled from lists furnished by each mission, is published from time to time. This generally includes the wives and adult daughters of the members of the missions. 領事官員另參加領事團，不參加外交團。主事僅

為各使館辦事人員，因非外交官，故不列名駐在國外交部主編之"外交官衙名錄" Diplomatic List.

Courier

在舊時代交通阻塞之情形下，本國政府與駐外使節傳遞消息極為不便，乃有書信使者或外交信差之派遣，一般對其身體及文書認為不可侵犯，應享有免除民刑事之權利。今日交通便利，有事時使節可拍發電報，向其本國政府請示，雖遠隔萬里，亦能朝發夕至，外交信差之用在通常情形之下逐漸減少。

Declaration

宣言而具有約束力者與國際間其他協定同，亦有創制國際法作用。亦有用以表明較小事件者。

另外有一種宣言無條約上之效力，僅為表示對某事之意見，或對某事加以解釋而已。

De facto recognition

如與新興國家或政府簽訂非條約性質之某種臨時或有限度目的之協定，如派遣領事官員等，皆屬事實承認如當叛亂政府在力量上能够治理一片領土，外國政府即予以事實承認，承認其為該地之統治者。此種事實承認為不確定的，為有限度的。對新興國家有先予以事實承認而後予以法律承認者。

De jure recognition

凡構成法律上之承認，必為與新興國家簽訂某種條約，或派遣使節駐紮於新興國家，或接受新興國家之使節來本國首都駐紮或正式發表對新興國家承認之聲明，此種承認為確定的，比較有永久性。

Démarche

此名辭頗難翻譯，在法文稱 faire une démarche 相等於英文之 make representations，包括步驟、建議、請求、嘗試、抗議、恐嚇、辦法、陳說等意義。

Diplomacy

外交乃以智慧與技巧，用商談方式，處理獨立國家間之國際關係。

大使在昔視爲"榮譽間諜" An honourable spy。在歐洲十六、七世紀時代，他們深信個人道德與公共道德爲兩事，所以十七世紀時出使威尼斯之英國大使 Sir Henry Wotton 曾謂"大使是一個誠實的人，國家爲着本身的利益，派他去國外說謊"。 An Ambassador is an honest man who is sent to lie abroad for the good of his country.

現今負責辦理國際間商談任務者，除大使等正式外交代表外，民主國家之總統、內閣總理或外交部長等亦參加外交談判。

Diplomatic pouches

外交郵袋爲國際間公認之制度，各國應互相尊重彼此之信譽，俾外交郵袋辦法不被濫用，此制在國際法與慣例上享有其特殊地位，公文遞送至外國時不受外國當局之檢查，但不得攜帶違禁物品或私人函件。

Diplomatic privilege

外交官正式派駐在外國，依照國際法其本人及家屬（包括配偶、子女及同居近親）與外交官同國籍之僕役等應享有下列各種特權，此種習慣由來已久，凡文明國家均一律遵行：

一、不可侵犯權 (Inviolability)——外交官代表國家，而國家在國際法上一律平等，不相侵犯，故外交官應享有不可侵犯權，如外交官個人身體自由不可侵犯，使館及外交官寓所以及車輛，檔案文書等皆不可侵犯，無論寓所之產權是否歸其政府所有，或由其出資租用，當地政府均應予以尊重，不得侵犯。如外交官濫用此種特權，庇護各種罪犯及使館以外之其他人員，則駐在國實無遵守之義務。

二、不受駐在國民刑事裁判權之管轄(Immunity from local civil and criminal jurisdiction)——爲便利外交官（包括館長及一切館員）行使職務起見，所有因公務而發生之民事案件，如債務損害契約等，駐在國法庭不能過問。又駐在國不得向外交官論罪科罰拘捕裁判，惟外交官對於當地法律公共安寧等均須遵守。

否則駐在國得迫令出境，如此自有礙本國體面。

三、不受財政法權之管轄（Exemption from taxation）──外交官對於駐在國一切租稅可以不納，但地方捐如住宅中之電燈自來水等，則屬於私人享受不能豁免。又如陰溝及街道之清潔，救火隊費用之分攤等，地方事業改進事項，外交官亦不能豁免。

關於外國使館僱用之僕役所享外交特權問題，國際法學者及各國慣例之見解與主張殊不一致，有主張不論國籍如何，凡在使館僱用時期，為便利外交官執行公務起見，當地政府一律給予僕役或車夫（包括駐在國本國國籍之僕役與車夫）應享之特權。反對此說者則謂凡本國國籍之僕役一律不應享受特權。亦有用互惠（Reciprocity）辦法者。

另一處理辦法，即本國籍之僕役或車夫解僱後，與外國使館無關，事後應受當地法權之管轄。

Diplomatic service 或 Foreign service

此詞可譯稱外交界，包括國內外的外交行政及職業外交官，為一永久組織。在1815年維爾納會議以前，無此項名稱。在昔使領館官員分為兩類，一類為服務駐外各大使館或公使館之外交官，稱為 Diplomatic service；一類為服務於駐外各級領事館之領事官，稱為 Consular service，彼此不能相互調用。今日各國多將兩類官員混合，稱為 Diplomatic service 或 Foreign service 兩類官員始可相互調用。

凡獨立國家皆可派遣，或接受外交官，是為國際公法所公認，無須依據條約訂定之。

Diplomatist

稱為外交官，與 diplomat 同，包括在國內外交部與駐外各使館及其他外交機構辦理外交事務的所有公務人員。

Doyen

英文稱 Dean，中文稱外交團團長，或領袖大使，為最高外交機構中年資最高之外交代表，如特命全權大使中駐在同一地之年資最老者擔任此職，其夫人稱爲 Doyenne。主要職責與典禮有關，爲皇宮或外交部傳達有關典禮消息，在公共場合代表外交團發言。如遇駐在國政府侵害外交團之特權與轄免權時，應即起而加以維護，或代表外交團向駐在國政府提出聯合之請求，或採取共同一致之行動。凡採取此項行動時，各使節均須事先獲得各自本國政府之訓令與批准。惟若干國家不贊同採取或接受此項共同行動。

Duck diplomacy

"水鳥外交"爲日本前駐華公使有吉明向日本外務省建議之對華外交政策，其意謂對華外交在表面上應取靜觀態度，以避免國際輿論之反響，實際上則屬行積極外交，以解決一切懸案，如水鳥之浮於水面，雖未見若何動作，而實際兩足則在水中積極撥動。

Ex aequo et bono

法庭裁判案件，不依照法律，而按照正義與良心。

According to what is just and good.

Excellency

對大使及公使各國皆尊稱„閣下"對民主國家元首或政府閣員等亦有尊稱"閣下"者，此項尊稱到1815年 Congress of Vienna 以後更爲普遍。

Exchange of Notes

此項換文多由外交部長代表其政府與駐在該國之關係國使節互換照會。負責簽署互換照會人員不必提供全權證書，但亦有規定事後須提經本國國會批准者。

Exequatur

爲政府承認外國領事之一種證書，允許新領事有權執行其領事職務，稱爲"領事證書"或"領事許可證"。

Ex officio

職務上 By virtue of one's official position.

Extradition

在甲國犯罪後逃至乙國，或在甲國犯罪,受審並判刑後逃至乙國，甲國可向乙國要求引渡，以便依法處辦。國家在法律上雖無引渡逃犯之義務，關於此類案件原則上現今有關國家多簽訂引渡條約，其辦法普通分爲兩種：（一）在條約上列舉犯罪之種類，（二）不在條約上列舉犯罪之種類，但聲明所犯罪行在兩國均須加以處辦時得要求引渡。亦有制定國內法列舉引渡之罪情，並規定引渡之程序者。

至政治犯一般國際法學者及各國政府多不接受引渡之要求。

Extraordinary

在昔外交官中之大使級分爲兩類，一類爲駐紮大使，即 Ordinary 大使。一類爲特命全權大使，即 Extraordinary 大使，乃奉本國政府命令辦理特殊任務者。但今日大使級外交官均一律稱爲特命全權大使。教皇所派使節與特命全權大使同一階級者，稱Papal Legates 或 Nuncios.

Fait accompli

未經合法手續，而以武力或其他手段造成侵犯他國之領土主權局面，稱之爲既成事實。

Fin de non-recevoir

在外交慣例中對對方之正式控訴和不滿，不加深究而予以拒絕。

Full Powers

如一國政府派遣代表與他國政府商訂條約等，或參與國際會議，其目的亦在簽訂條約，依照國際慣例，派遣國政府應對代表頒發證書，授與全權，此項文書稱爲全權證書。即大使公使奉本國政府命，出任特別交涉，或參加國際會議達成簽訂條約之目的者，亦須由本國政府另頒全權證書，以便出席。

　　全權證書有賦與有限權限及無限權限之分。事實上今日因交通電信便利，一國政府很少給予使者以無限權限，且批准權係政府大權，由政府保留，故條約簽訂後，仍須呈由本國政府最後批准。

　　條約簽訂前，代表應將全權證書相互校閱。如爲國際會議，則事先另組一委員會負責辦理校閱事宜。

Good offices

凡遇兩國因事發生爭辯或戰爭時，雙方間直接談判，事實上已無法解決問題，乃經由一方或雙方之請求，或自願出面調停，第三國常參預談判俾雙方能趨於和解。此處所謂第三國參預調停，僅將衝突雙方拉攏使其再行直接談判之意，與 Mediation 之實際由第三國參加商談者不同。

Habeas corpus

召被拘禁者至法庭之命令，或無罪釋放之命令，或由一法庭移送人犯至他法庭之文書。A writ for delivering a person from false imprisonment, or for removing a person from one court to another.

Honorary consul

在未設領事之地，爲發展該地之本國商業及保護居留之僑胞計，得設名譽領事，由居留該地之僑民，或所在國人民，或有關外籍人士中選任之。

Inter alia

其中 Among other things. These provisions declare, inter alia, that…………

International usage

國際間所發生之例行習慣，經多數國家之明示或默許，漸漸成爲國際法源或法則，而爲國際間相互遵守者，謂之爲國際慣例。

Inter se

在彼等自己中 Between or among themselves.

Ipso facto

就事論事 By that very deed or fact. In the fact itself.

Laisser-passer

政府官員因公出國旅行，或外交官赴任，除携帶護照外，尚須請擬前往旅行國家之使領館頒發一放行文書，以免其海關對行李之查驗。

Lettre de Cabinet

爲君主對君主之國書，不及 Lettre de Chancellerie 之正式與嚴格，後者爲君主對民主國家總統之國書，此類實例以英國宮廷最多。

Mise en demeure

甲政府向乙政府率直提出"接受或不接受"之要求時，謂之 m.e.d.

Modus vivendi

"臨時協定"乃兩國短期之妥協，凡關係國對某項問題一時妥協，而防將來有所變更，故成立臨時協定，日後如可能時再簽訂正式條約。

Note verbale

爲接近"節略"之一種外交文書，不如"照會"之嚴格，但較"備忘錄"爲正式，僅記載質問及談話之要點。此項公文不簽名，但在文末可加習慣之客氣語。

Open diplomacy 與 Secret diplomacy

公開外交爲對秘密外交而言，即國際間之條約協定以及談判諒解等外交活動，均須公開爲之。條約簽訂後，尤須送經聯合國登記，登記後始能生效。

依照聯合國憲章第一百零二條規定："一 本憲章發生效力後，聯合國任何會員國所締結之一切條約及國際協定，應儘速在秘書處登記，並由秘書處公佈之。二、當事國對於未經依本條第一項規定登記之條約或國際協定，不得向聯合國任何機關援引之"。

在昔舊式外交手段，以爲欲使軍事協定或軍事同盟功成奏效，必須使其嚴守秘密，使敵國不知對方之實力與內幕。今日一般多贊成公開之民主外交，對秘密外交加以責難，如外交在秘密中進行，徒引起國內外人士之猜疑。

Papal Legate 與 Nuncio

教皇派遣之大使級外交官分爲兩類；一爲 Papal Legate，多由樞機主教 (Cardinal) 擔任；一爲 Papal Nuncio，非由樞機主教擔任。兩者皆相當於各國所派之全權大使，辦理精神上及宗教上事務，駐在外國與其他國家所派外交代表同享外交官之特權與榮譽。

依照 1815 年 Règlement de Vienne 第四條規定，Nuncio 視爲駐在國外交團團長。1856年英國正式解釋謂，維爾納會議時，既准教廷代表之席位高於其他同等之外交代表，而不管其到任日期之先後，此慣例應不容變更，此說至今仍維持有效。事實上在天主教國家，對教皇精神上之力量特別尊重，即無維爾納會議之規定，各國對教廷大使，因基於禮讓，亦多予以榮譽之地位。

教廷外交官除上述者外，尚有相當於公使級之Internuncio，亦尊稱爲 His Excellency，其教廷公使館稱爲 Apostolic Internunciature。

Per se

就事論事，本身的 By itself.

Persona Grata

Persona grata 原意爲 popular character。如使節之行爲與言論不受當地政府歡迎，駐在國政府即不再認該使爲相宜之外交代表 Persona grata，該使即成爲不相宜之外交代表 Persona non grata. 若被如此宣佈，等於向該使原來派遣國政府要求撤回。

Prendre acte 與 Donner acte

Acte 一詞在外交上適用於任何獲得協議之文書，與英文 act 或 Instrument 一詞類似。Prendre acte 與英文 Take note of 相近似，有承認意，無異說 I shall take note of this and bring it up against you in the future.

Donner acte 即對對方所作之行爲予以承認。

Prima facie

表面，驟視之 At first sight.

Prima-facie evidence

形跡上之證據，若不反對，則足生效力之證據。

Evidence sufficient in law to raise a presumption of fact or establish the fact in question unless rebutted.

Pro and Con

贊成與反對，詳細之討論。In plural, pros and cons.

Procès Verbal

會議紀錄，英文稱爲 Minutes，爲外交談判及決議之紀錄。在各種重要會議中均由秘書處於每次會議後準備一會議錄，說明開會日期，時間，地點及參與會議各國代表等姓名，同時記載會議內容及結論。此項會議錄通常由擔任會議之主席及秘書長簽名，如屬更重要會議，則須與會各代表簽署。

Pro formâ

爲形式之故 For form's sake merely to satisfy rules.

Pro tempore

暫時 Temporarily, for a short time.

Protest

外交代表有保護本國種種權利與榮譽，以及本國人民生命財產之責，如此項權益遭受侵害，不管對方政府曾否直接從事此項侵損他人之行爲，皆應對此項行爲負其責任，受損害之一方得提出抗議，並要求賠償。

如駐在國政府所行所爲有損派駐該國使領館人員之生命財產，或使領館應享各項特權，有關使館有權向駐在國政府提出抗議，外交團領袖大使有維護各使館應享特權之責，亦得代表有關使館採取行動，向駐在國政府提出抗議。

Protocol

爲國際協定之一種，中文稱爲議定書，凡較條約或專約略欠正式之協定，多採用議定書形式。議定書可以修正多邊的國際協定。雙邊條約亦常附議定書以補充或修正原先經雙方簽訂之條約。

凡遇多邊條約或專約簽訂後，如需要以宣言或其他協定增補，以說明條約本身文字者，得再簽 Final Protocol，而該增補之議定書可以視條約本身之一部份。

Quid pro quo

交換物，有來有往。An equivalent in return.

Raison d'État

國家利益高於一切私人道德的外交與政治理論。

Ratification

雙邊條約簽訂後，必須分別經由雙方簽字國元首,依照憲法程序，予以批准並互換批准書。

　　如爲多邊條約，原約本由簽約所在國政府保管，其他各簽約國各得副本一份備查。各國批准存放手續,則依照條約規定辦理。

Rebus sic stantibus

因某種情勢簽訂條約，如經國際法庭宣佈情勢變遷,條約卽失效，簽約國卽不再受此約之拘束。

Representations

有譯爲建議者，乃外交官向駐在國政府一種應行之步驟，目的在請求該國政府對某項問題重加考慮。

Reservation

"保留"一詞，在國際法內乃一國對於國際所行條約之價值，予以限制或消滅之意。其效力之發生，以他國之同意爲必要之條件，按慣例多爲默示的，不必强要某國之明示同意。

　　比如一國願意加入某條約，但因該約中某條或某數條款措詞關係，不敢貿然加入,在此種情形下可對某條或某數條提出保留，此可在簽約時爲之，正式載入會議紀錄，或在批准時爲之。

Safe-conduct

甲乙兩國絕交後，甲國外交官欲通行乙國領土，乙國在普通情況下仍核發通行證，准其通行。

Severance of Diplomatic Relations

甲國對乙國因事極表不滿,外交方面之交涉調處已無法解決問題，而增進邦交，乃多採取斷絕外交關係關閉使館辦法，兩國雖不卽使用武力，一方既已採取此種行動，亦認爲極端嚴重。

較斷絕邦交略輕之事件，則爲暫時撤退甲國駐乙國之外交使節，而將其使館交由一低級之館員臨時代理館務。

Sine die

無限，不限期 Indefinitely, without fixing any future date.

Sine quâ non

緊要之物 An essential without which it is impossible to come to terms.

Speech*

此爲新大使或公使到任時向駐在國元首呈遞其到任國書時所致之頌詞，首先由該使節表示奉派出使之愉快，繼轉達其本國元首對駐在國元首致敬及親善之意，又表示其本人願努力促進兩國間之友好關係。如新使以往曾在駐在國之本國使館擔任參事秘書等職，亦不妨在頌詞中追述過去居留之快慰心情。

> * 頌詞之英文譯名頗多，有 speech, address, message, greeting message 等之不同，但在 Satow 之 A Guide to Diplomatic Practice (4th Edition, pp. 145–148)書中則稱爲 speech，故取法之。

Status quo

現狀，表示在某特定時間之狀況或情勢。The position in which affairs actually are; the present situation of affairs.

Theory of Reciprocity

國際間締結通商條約，或施行其他通商政策時，締約國基於國家利益，以相互交換通商上均等利益爲原則之主義。根據互惠主義而訂立之條約，謂之"互惠條約" (Reciprocity Treaty).

Treaty

條約形式較莊嚴，爲政府間達成協定之一種正式文書，有拘束力，條約有雙邊與多邊之分，如爲雙邊條約，兩國文字可並書，每一國可以保有原簽字約本一份。由甲國持有者，則甲國文字印於乙國文字之前，甲國全權代表之名列於乙國代表之前，並首先簽字。如原簽字約本由乙國保有，則乙國文字印在甲國文字之前，代表簽字等亦在前。

　　如爲多邊條約，其列名及簽字等則完全依照輪替辦法辦理。

Ultimatum

　　"最後通牒"又直譯爲"哀的美敦書"，爲在談判正式破裂前，甲國政府或其外交代表向乙國提出最後條件，限乙國在一定時間內必須作明確迅速之答復。使用此辭普通包含使用武力之恫嚇，如條件被乙國拒絕，則兩國邦交可能斷絕，或兩國發生戰事，或其他不幸事件。

Viva voce

　　口說 Orally, as opposed to in writing.

二、尊　稱

Titles of Courtesy

1. 教皇（Pope）

   Most Holy Father （法文稱 Très-Saint Père, 或 Très-Vénérable Père, 或 Vénérable）Holiness or Your Holiness（Sainteté, 或 Béatitude）

   希臘教之大主教亦尊稱 Beatitude, 如稱 His Beatitude the Patriarch.

2. 國王或皇帝（Kings of Emperors）

   Sire, Your Majesty, Majesty （法文稱 Votre Majesté, 或 Majesté）

   王或皇后稱 Madame

   國君在公事上相互稱呼為 Sir My Brother, 或法文 Monsieur Mon Frère. 對王或皇后則稱 Madame My Sister, 或法文 Madame Ma Soeur.

3. 王或皇太子（Prince）

   Royal Highness, Imperial Highness（Altesse Royale, Altesse Impériale, Monseigneur）, Highness（Altesse）. 公主仿照王子之尊稱。

4. 總統（President）

   Mr. President（Monsieur le Président）

   Excellency（Excellence）

5. 總理（Prime Minister）

   Excellency, 在英國尊稱 The Right Honourable.

   總督（Governor-General）亦尊稱 Excellency.

6. 外交部長及其他部長級官員（Minister for Foreign Affairs and other Cabinet Ministers）

Mr. Minister, Excellency, The Right Honourable, (Monsieur le Ministre, Excellence) 對美國閣員宜尊稱 The Honorable.

7. 大使或公使 (Ambassador or Minister)

Mr. Ambassador (Monsieur l'Ambassadeur), Excellency (Excellence), Your Excellency (Votre Excellence). 對美國使節宜尊稱 The Honorable.

8. 樞機主教 (Cardinal)

His Eminence the Cardinal Secretary of State.

中華社會科學叢書

實用外交文牘 (增訂本)
PRACTICAL DIPLOMATIC CORRESPONDENCE (REVISED EDITION)

作　　者／劉振鴻　編著
主　　編／劉郁君
美術編輯／本局編輯部

出 版 者／中華書局
發 行 人／張敏君
副總經理／陳又齊
行銷經理／王新君　林文鶯
地　　址／11494 台北市內湖區舊宗路二段181巷8號5樓
客服專線／02-8797-8396　　傳　真／02-8797-8909
網　　址／www.chunghwabook.com.tw
匯款帳號／華南商業銀行　　西湖分行
　　　　　179-10-002693-1　中華書局股份有限公司

法律顧問／安侯法律事務所
製版印刷／維中科技有限公司　海瑞印刷品有限公司
出版日期／2021年1月三版
版本備註／據1971年2月二版復刻重製
定　　價／NTD 350

國家圖書館出版品預行編目（CIP）資料

實用外交文牘 = Practical diplomatic
　correspondence/劉振鵬(CharLes P. Liu)編. ──
　三版. ── 臺北市 ：中華書局, 2021.01
　　面 ； 公分. ── (中華社會科學叢書)
　ISBN 978-986-5512-41-5(平裝)

1.英語 2.外交 3.應用文
805.179　　　　　　　　　　　　　　109019567